Ferdinant P. Simon

Antony and Hero

Volume 1

Ferdinant P. Simon

Antony and Hero
Volume 1

ISBN/EAN: 9783337194314

Printed in Europe, USA, Canada, Australia, Japan

Cover: Foto ©Andreas Hilbeck / pixelio.de

More available books at **www.hansebooks.com**

ANTONY AND HERO

— BY —

SIMMIE.

F. Simon, Publisher.

NEW HAVEN, CONNECTICUT.

1899.

POETICAL SELECTIONS.

Hero's description of sunrise. Act 1, Scene 1.

Why, I was awake, and
In serious meditation, an hour before
O'er eastern mountains in it's distant orb,
The sun arose in fiery majesty,
And was admiring how the sparkling dew
Did grace the changing landscape hereabouts,
As sol's slow creeping fire did burnish every drop.

Antony's praise of ambition. Act 1, Scene 1.

Well has he succeeded
In his fight for fame, and I am proud of
His acquaintance. Well do I remember,
How in our youthful sports, he ever did
Affect commanding, a leadership
Was always his ambition, and on that
He has built a monument of fame. I
Was ever known for and proud of my strength,
And age made that youthful pride a serious
Ambition till I became an athlete.
A man's life is modeled out in youth
By an unseen power, and as he dies
So was it destined.

Alice trying to encourage Leopole. Act 1, Scene 3.

Come Leopole, be merry,
This sullenness does not become you, and
You have no cause for being so. One defeat
Is no disgrace, not when your victories
Are summed up. 'Twas an honor to be matched
To Antony. Come let's be merry as usual.

Antony's praise of uniforms. Act 2, Scene 1.

Oh such a specticle! Look! Look! He was wise,
Who first suggested uniforms for soldiers,
For while formidable to the enemy,
They inspire a friend. Look! See how more imposing
Than the citizens, and yet they are but people.
                    And this martial music,
Makes one almost wish for foes.

Hero's defense of Antony. Act 2, Scene 1.

'Tis false,
I swear it! I have been his inmost friend
For many years, and have oft heard him praise
Your qualities and ambition. He was
The first to applaud your every promotion,
Of all your friends he was most eager to hear from you,
And good news he would address as though
Your person with : Brave Charles with but a few
More strides we shall say Great Charles ! 'Twas he
Suggested, as my father knows, 'all these
New entertainments for to-day, and he
Worked for their completion so inceasingly,
There was no time for conspiring. And now
You call him your enemy, and a traitor,
For this small accident that only seemed to harm.

Hero's love for Antony. Act 2, Scene 3.

Think you I would encourage a man, who
Downed my Antony ? No ! If Antony dies,
Why so do I to all the world.
I would live and die a dry old spinster
With no occupation, but training flowers
For his monument.

Antony's generosity and confidence in his friends. Act 4, Scene 1.

No, No. You live,
Live and be famous, live and be honored
As an athlete, for the people must have one
For their amusement and their idol, and
Who is there but you that is worthy, and
Entitled to their praise? And, Leopole,
All the medals and trophys I have won,
I've willed to you, they with my titles
When I am dead are yours, with my best wishes
That you honor them, and there is no one
More confident than I am that you will.

CAST.

Antony,—Champion Athlete.

Charles,—A Duke's Officer,

Leopole,—Ex-Champion Athlete,

Abraham,—Judge and Hero's Father,

Wiggins,—Jailor,

Swipes,—His Assistant,

Tom Sawyer,—
Bill Judson,— } Tough Characters.

Johnson,—Prosecutor,

Jones,—Sheriff,

Hero,—Antony's Love,

Margaret,—Antony's Sister,

Theresa,—Hero's Maid,

Alice,—A Cortizan,

Citizens, Officers, Band, Soldiers.

Act I. (Scene 1.) *Abraham discovered.*

Abraham.—Now has father time began that day, which crowns
My happiness, and brought sol's glowing light
O'er eastern mountain tops to do his part.
Oh happiness to think, my daughter weds
To-day, and weds a man that's loved by men.
What luck of fortune what anything brings
More joy to a loving father, there's nothing.
It has brought youth back to my mind, but not
My bones, for if it had I'ld dance and leap,
And somersault for joy. But no, mine must
Be expressed with pleased appearances. She
Will wed Antony ere night, Antony
The famous athlete,
He who so lately conquered Leopole,
The favorite of the duke his chum, called
Hercules by all, and praised above him
All for his qualities,
Untill Antony o'erthrew him as though
He had no opposition and many
Claim 'twas so for policy to lure some
Spicy wager on another trial.
No, no!
That desperate aspect such tugging and
Straining that every muscle seemed to swell
An inch, that red complexion as when
Exertion crowds a man's blood against his
Skin and forces out large beads of sweat, such
Heaveing at the finish to catch his breath
All prove that Leopole was not trifeling.
I'll not believe it. I have double cause
For joy, for to-day I will be relieved
Of my political cares for brave Charles,
A chum of Antony's as boys,
But seperated these five years by their
Professions to seek fame and fortune, and
Well they have succeeded, Antony the
Mighty athlete and Charles the brave soldier.

'T will be a sight to see those famous leaders
In their callings meet, with their mutual love
Since childhood.   Charles fame and qualities,
Have won for him succession to my office,
Which he comes to-day to accept, and I
Will be relieved.   But ho ! Come, come, be merry.
            (*Rings for and enter servant.*)
Where's Hero, not up yet !   Go make her stir.
                (*Exit servant.*)
The day's and hour gone.   She must be
Much contented to sleep so long this day.
                (*Enter Hero.*)

Hero.—Good morning.   Did you think me tardy?

Abr.—You are not much interested in your
Marrying or you'd been about ere this.

Hero.—   Why. I was awake and in
Serious meditation, an hour before
O'er eastern mountains in his distant orb
The sun arose in fiery majesty.
And was admiring how the sparkling dew
Did grace the changing landscape hereabouts,
As sol's slow creeping fire did burnish every drop.

Abr.—You should be gay and happy, this is no time
For seriousness —

Hero.—   But my future happiness
Is a serious question.

Abr.—   It was.
But with such a husband as Antony
To care for that you should be merry.

Hero.—It always was my nature to be serious
And I thank my maker for that fault.   I
Would not for the world be giddy, for then
I'ld not have Antony's love.

Abr.—The happiness that comes from love lies not,
As some claim, all in the procuring, there's
More in the preserving.   And if you would
Keep fresh your husbands love, take these receipts
From my experience.

First, do not be dominering, for heaven
Decreed that woman should not equal man.
Think more of comforting your husband, than
Of teaching him, and if in aught you think
He's wrong and cannot change him with
A sort of suplicating modest way,
Convince yourself he's right. In cleanliness,
In order, yea in everything be so precise
As to consider all your imperfections,
As transgressions. 'Tis the duty of
The husband to furnish means of sustainance
For his family. 'Tis the duty of
The wife to use those means to best advantage,
For both the happiness and comfort of
Her family. You are both worthy of each other
Which is much towards making your love mutual.

Hero.—My father, glad I am to be advised
By anyone with more experience,
And you can be content these maxims shall
For reference ever be, deep graven in
My memory. (*Enter Leo.*)

Leo.—Good morrow both, and happy day.

Hero.—Good morrow, Leopole.

Abr.—Good morrow to you, and your looks proclaim,
A wish of happiness unnecessary.

Leo.—I have good cause for happiness for I
Come direct from your successor. The first
I saw of him in five long years.

Abr.— How does
He look and how behave himself amongst
His honors? Glad to be back no doubt.

Leo.— Tall and handsome but
A little stiff to me as though to say,
My position sir, calls for respect.

Hero.— 'Tis
Conceitedness, 'tis natural to him,
He was so as a boy.

Leo.— Prepare
To welcome him for he'll be here ere long
On business. He wished me to remind you,
To make all preparations for the parade.

Abr.—'Twas unnecessary. The paraders
Will be ready when we are. We shall march
About and arrive at the tribunal
So as to install him at high noon when
My term expires.

Leo.— He is anxious to have
Much celebration.

Abr.— The preparations
Are the grandest I've yet known. (*Exit Abr. enter Theresa.*)

Ther.—Oh Hero Antony is coming.
Good morrow Leopole.

Leo.— Good morrow.

Hero.—He is coming for us, for there's a good view
From his porch of this parade to which we
Are invited. I'll go prepare myself
For·I promised to be waiting for him. (*Exit Hero.*)

Ther.—Happy are they for they'll be man and wife
Ere night.

Leo.— I envy Antony.

Ther.— All men do
That know her. But here he comes and his sister to.
(*Enter Ant., Marg.*)

Ant.—Good morrow.

Leo.—Good morrow Antony.

Ther.—Good morrow Antony and Margaret.

Marg.—Good morrow both.

Ant.—Love must be contagious for
These private interviews mean nothing else.

Ther.—Oh I've oft heard of two diseases
Whose symptoms were alike.

Ant.— Where's my partner
In this sickness? We'll groan, and heave, and make
A hospital of this room.

Marg.— And I'll be
All your physicians.

Ant.— No, no. The disease
Is very contagious, and your none
To vigorous to catch it.

Marg.— Yes, I see
It effects even those who are famous
For their strength.

Ant.—Well how goes it with Leopole?

Marg.—I see it effects even those, who are
Famous for their strength.

Ant.—I admit. But how is Leopole?

Leo.—Oh fairly well. I've just come from Charles.

Ant.—How is he? He must have come this morning
For I looked for him last night. But has he changed?

Leo.—You'll see him soon yourself, for he'll be here
Before the parade.

Ant.—A five year's seperation of two such palls.
You cannot imagine how this meeting 's
Looked for. But how does he look, as large as I?

Leo.—Tall and handsome with a military brace.

Ant.— Well has he succeeded
In his fight for fame, and I am proud of
His acquaintance. Well I do remember,
How in our youthful sports, he ever did
Affect commanding, a leadership
Was always his ambition. And on that
He has built a monument of fame. I,
Was ever known for and proud of my strength,
And age made that youthful pride, a serious
Ambition till I became an athlete.
· A man's life is modeled out in youth
By an unseen power and as he dies,
So was it destined. But no more lecturing (*Enter Hero.*)
For here's a better subject. Good morrow.

Hero.—Good morrow Antony. I see you're here.

Ant.—I wish I had been these last few hours, I'ld a
    Rid myself of them, for it tortured me
    To think that father time kept us apart.

Marg.—I will leave, the disease is very catching,
    And I must not expose myself being frail.

Ther.—I'll go to.   (*Exit Marg., Ther.*)

Leo.—   I'll go have a consultation
    With your father.   (*Exit Leo.*)

Hero.—   What new styled bickering
    Is this?

Ant.—   Theresa and Leopole were
    At some private conversation as we
    Entered. I proclaimed it a sign of love,
    They turned the joke on me, and made love in me
    A contagious disease. And love so would
    I have it with you alone as my physician
    And have you catch it.

Hero.—   Why so it is Antony.

Ant.—As we have our wishes we must be happy.
                (*He embraces her, she takes a tie from him.*)

Hero.—This will I keep.

Ant.—   I cannot be without it
    From here to home.

Hero.—   You must.

Ant.—I'll not. (*Goes to take it from her. Enter Leo.*)

Leo.—   Hem, Hem.
    Let the patient enter the consultation.
    Come Anthony you are wanted.

Ant.—Give me my tie.

Hero.—No, No. My father is waiting. (*Exit Ant. Leo.*) I'll
    Not give it to him. I'll hide it. But where ?
    I'll make a garter of it and let him
    Take it off to-night for then I'll be his wife
    And t'will please him. Oh Antony in my eyes
    Thou alone of all men art to be loved. (*Ties on the garter*)
    Tis quite a novel way of pleasing him,
    But I guess he'll not think less of me for it. (*Enter Char.*)

Oh Charles, welcome.   This is a gala day,
From all quarters.   Glad I am you have returned

Char.—It does feel good to be amongst the old
Familiar scenes and faces once again.

Hero.)—It seems more than an age since you left.
You will remain amongst us now I hope.

Char.—Yes I will remain among those I love.

Hero.—How was it abroad, did you like it ?

Char.—Anything that I could wish for was mine,
But that is naught, wealth, station, fame or sport
All are nothing without love, that I had
Left behind.

Hero.—Were there no friends or ladies there
That you admired ?

Char.—No, No.   They say, man truly loves but once.

Hero.—And was your love here?

Char.—   Yes Hero.

Hero.—   And why
Did you not send for her ?

Char.—Would she have come ?

Hero.—Why sure she would, if she loved you.

Char.—   Hero,
Can't you see, 'tis you I mean, 'tis you I love.
'Tis for you I've pined these five long years.
            (*He embraces her.   Marg. appear and exit.*)

Hero.—Then you must learn to forget me.   I spoke
But as a friend to you, not thinking you'ld
Take this privelege.   You know I never
Loved you even as a boy.   Besides, I will
Be Anthony's bride ere night.

Char.—   What !   You'll marry
Antony, that drone, who dares no further
Than calling distance from his mother ?

Hero.—Save yourself and tell him so.

Char.—   No !   I'll not
Speak as much to him.

Hero.—   I thought so. but
You would were he a woman, brave soldier.

Char.—T'was not in fear I spoke but in honor,
I am no more within his sphere,
No, nor ever was, As a boy I used
His company for pastime.

Hero—   And he used you
As a mop for pastime.

Char.—   With his strength he did,
But of that the ignorant have the most,
And such he is, born to sleep and rot
In his mother's lap, while I went about
The world and fought through fire and smoke for fortune
And a name.

Hero.—   In sham battles you might have,
For you never were where courage alone
Would bring you. If I had Antony's name,
I would not trade for yours, besides, I'd rather
Have him just plain body and soul, than you
With all the polishings from titles
Ever bestowed.

Char.—   My business now is with
Your father. Will you call him ?

Hero.— ·   I believe,
He is coming. (*Enter Ant. Leo. Abr. following.*)

Ant.—If ever a man did die of ecstasy I will to-day,
Why Charles, how are you? (*Reaches out his hand. Chas.
coldly salutes.*)

Char. to Hero.—   I have business with
Your father.

Hero.—   Antony, I
Have oft been told, that they who inherit
Fame or fortune, use either like fools would
Through ignorance of the way,
Now I believe it. (*Char. Abr. Leo. converse.*)

Ant.—It cannot be he's grown so proud. No, Hero,
He has been through much excitement the last

Few days which has quite unnerved him, when that
Is settled he will regret this, and I'll
Forgive him.

Hero.—   Perhaps. But
You should remember he was ever so.

Ant.—Well, forget that now and give me my tie.

Hero.—No, I will not.

Ant.—   You must, I cannot venture
From here to home without it.

Hero.—You must, for I cannot give it to you now.

Ant.—And why not?

Hero.—   Never mind, I will get you
One of my father's.

Ant.—   And why not my own ?
Tell me.

Hero.—   I'll not, another is as good.

Ant.—I must know why not my own.

Hero.—Well, if you must know, it is my garter,
And let it be till you yourself this night
Remove it, for then we will be wedded.

Ant.—A kiss and it's a bargain. (*They kiss.*)

Hero.—   And
If any man can show you it ere night,
I will not deny he has seduced me.

Ant.—And I will hold you to your word.

Char. aside.—I would give my office for that tie.

Hero.—   Come
We'll after Theresa and Margaret
And prepare us for the parade. (*Exit both.*)

Char.—   Now all's
Complete for our exchanging offices
This noon.

Abr.—I have for weeks been getting ready,
Wait, I will get the papers. (*Exit Abr.*)

Char.—   Leopole.
You are jealous of this Antony, who
Conquered you by accident, and who now
Wears your honors. He who is looked at
As a hero, while you are passed by but
As a common man. Say that you are.

Leo.—   Well,
No doubt I'd like the honors, but he earned them.

Char.—But you can have them, and I will help you
Get them and pay you well for what you do
Towards getting them. I would rather see you
Than he looked up to.

Leo.—I would have to conquer him ere they'ed be mine.

Char.—I say no. Listen, you are a friend
Of Theresa, Hero's maid.

Leo.—   Yes.

Char.—   Well.
Hero wears a necktie as a garter,
Get that for me and I will make you rich,
And honored. With Theresa's help you can.
No questions now, do as I bid and I'll
Do as I said, make you rich and honored.

Leo.—I would do anything to be again
In favor.

Char.—They are in there, go do your best
To get that tie, 'tis worth a fortune. (*Enter Abr. Leo
                                   starts out.*)

Abr.—Here are the papers.
                    (*Scene closes.*)

(Scene 2.) *A Street.*

(Enter jagged citizens from one side.   Bill from the other.)

1st Cit.—Hurra ! These sporting days don't come often. Come we will have another drink.

Bill.—What cronicaled event has earned this holiday?

1st Cit.—Well, if here ain't Bill and jollying as usual. Come make up the party, we're in for a good time. Are you with us ?

Bill.—And where are you making for ?

1st Cit.—To the Cobweb first, then to see the parade. Are you with us ?

Bill.—Am I with you? Well I guess. But say, is Tom going ?

1st Cit.—Why, sure Tom is with us.

Bill.—Then count me out, then count me out. I am above his company.

Tom.—Now what is there about me causes this dislike ?

Bill.—Oh, that headlight, that boquet on your face.

Tom.—Why, I bought that myself, and all else that I wear.

Bill—You forgot, those clothes there're from my last donation day. I will have to have another, you begin to look seedy. Next Monday, Tom.

Tom.—You talk of donating. All you own that's not on your back is security for your board.

1st Cit. — No more boys, for here comes Charles, the newly elected. *(Enter Charles.)*

Bill, Tom, Cit.—Hurra ! for Charles.

Char. salutes.—Tanks friends, come have a drink.

Cit.—Certainly.

Bill.—With pleasure.

Tom.—At your service.

Bill.—That tickles us, ay Tom ?

Tom.—A good man for the office, the election should come oftener.

Char.—Come everybody. *(Exit Char.)*

Tom.—That's unnecessary coaxing. (*Exit Tom, Bill.*)

1st Cit.— A wise man is Charles, now we shall have good judging.

2d Cit.—Wise he is, and we shall.

1st Cit.—He looked wise.

2d Cit.—He did that.

1st Cit.—Did you note how little he said, and how stern he looked, and how he did salute. That's wisdom, that's learning. Now you have seen a great man.

2d Cit. — Ay.

1st Cit.—But come, we'll be with them. (*Exit Citizens.*)

(*Scene closes*))

(Scene 3.)   *A Barroom.*

(*Leo. and Alice discovered.*)

Alice.—   Come, Leopole be merry,
This sullenness does not become you and
You have no cause for being so.   One defeat
Is no disgrace, not when your victories
Are summed up.   'Twas an honor to be matched
To Antony.   Come, let's be merry as usual.

Leo.—Go 'way, you pratting fool.   'Twas such as you
Caused my defeat, you, who make the fortunate
Your victims, and prey on them so long
As they have money, then cast them off for others,
Go way, I say.   I cast you off
Before I'm so far gone that you'll cast me.

Alice.—Oh I'm not so sorry as you thought I'ld be,
But I'll get even with you for this.
                    (*Enter Char., Bill, Tom., Cit., they go to the bar.*)

All.—Hurrah for Charles.

Char.—Come what will it be? (*They drink.*)

Leo.—Such is fortune's greeting no man gets it.
My fortune got it once but
Both have left me.   Why are there two such words
As fortune and favour?

One is superfluous, they mean the same,
They are inseperable, no man has
Either, they come and go together as
Natural, as heat and cold to summer
And winter. They are what all are after
But few get, and no man seeks them singly.
'Tis misery to want them, 'tis misery
To have them, and yet they're wanted. They were
Mine once but they escaped me, and now I
Seek again. Charles will aid me if I will
Be false to Antony who has so much
Befriended me. Who would not if they could
By crooked by-ways come to fortune, if
Naught but poeple's opinion were the punishment?
None but the simple.
And they alone for want of reason, would doubt
The outcome of a chance. I'll not be such.
I will do anything to be again
With fortune and with favour. Who is there
That has had a leadership o'er his companions,
An assendancy o'er all, could endure
Being common and with my chance? Oh fame,
Why is thy charm so strong? Why is thy yield
So great? Why is the entrance to your domain
So complicated, and yet to seem so simple?
Art thou the curse from heaven to Adam?

Bill.—Hurra! He has our voices. None before
Him was as good, ay Tom?

Tom.—Hurra! He's in my favour.

Cit's.—Hurra! (*Char. comes to Leo.*)

Char.—Well Leopole, why so gloomy? Come have one.

Leo.—   I'm gloomy for your good
And mine. 'Tis brooding harm to Antony
Makes me so.

Char.—Yes, we must down him, and that
To-day. No doubt he'll be a spectator
To the parade from his house. If some accident
Should happen there, and blame him for it?

Leo.—He'll view it from his porch and that is lined
With cobbles. If one of them could be pushed off
While he is there ? (*Alice listening.*)

Char.—And as I pass. Do that
And your fortune will return. (*They whisper.*) (*Bill,*
Tom, Citizens shaking dice.)

Bill.—'Twas a duce.

Tom.—'Twas a six.

Bill.—'Twas a duce.

Tom.—'Twas a six I say. Afraid you'll get stuck ?

Bill.—No, you loggerheaded fool, but I'll not get cheated.

Tom.—Who's a loggerheaded fool ?

Bill.—You ! (*They fight, Citizens try to stop them.*)

Cit.—Come, stop, be friends. Bill, Tom, stop !

Proprietor. — Go outside for such business. I'll have no dis-
turbance in my place. (*Rushes them out.*)

Leo.—And what is your motive
In downing Antony ?

Char.— You know Hero,
Whom he is to wed to-day ? I wished her
For myself, but she this morning snubbed me
And went to praising Antony so
She must have broken my gall, and I'll never
Rest easy if they are happy.

Leo.—What does the tie in this ?

Char.— Did you get it ?

Leo.—No, but I will, for I have bargained with Theresa
To procure it, and what I wish she'll do.

Char.— Then get it
Without fail, for with that I'll torture him
If nothing more. Well, I must away. Don't fail
But have an accident before his house.

Leo.—I will try all possible means to.

Alice.— And I
Will try all possible means to stop you.

Char.—Who is this thing ?

Alice.—This thing is what knows all your plans.

Char.—What, spying on us ?

Alice.—No, accidently overheard.

Char.—You lie. You have been spying.

Alice.—And if I have, what of it ?

Char.—Yes, what of it, even if you did hear all we said ?

Alice.—Oh, I might bother you a bit, if I
    See Antony first.

Chor.—You bother us, you fallen witch,
    One word from me would lock you up for months.

Alice.—Then say the word and lock me up, if you can,
    But I'll do some mischief first, and you can blame
    Him for it. I have befriended him
    In all I could for more than a year, and
    Now he turns me off as trash and blames me
    For his misfortune. Leopole, that was
    A dose of poison to me, rank poison,
    And it will take something rank to drive it out.
    I will bring your plans to Antony, that
    May relieve me some. So Good-Bye. I'll see
    Whether you'll wear his honors or not. (*Starts to go.*)

Char.—Stop her. (*Leo stops her.*)
    We'll keep you from harm until you are harmless. (*To
    proprietor.*) Have you a room we can lock her in for a few
    hours ?

Prop.—Right here. Bring her in.

Char.—I've never been fooled by man, so I'll not let woman start
    it. Put her in there ! (*Alice fights and screams.*) (*To
    prop.*) Let her out in a couple of hours.
             Now, Leopole,
    I will go meet the procession. You go
    To Antony's, and don't fail or weaken
    In our plans, for there's much for you to gain,
    And my revenge.
            (*Scene closes.*)

Act II. *Before Antony's Home.*

(Citizens discovered lined up like viewing a parade.)

(Enter Tom, Bill and Citizens.)

Bill.—We'll find no better place, let's wait here until they have passed.

Tom.—'Twill be a long wait without a drink. Keep moving, we'll meet some place to stop in. It's better than standing here.

Bill.—You've got a good load aboard now, let that settle, then you'll have time and room for another.

Tom.—Your load must bother you that you refuse.

Bill.—I have a little sense.

Tom.—I never saw you pass a barroom when you had cents enough to buy a drink.

Bill.—You never got that blossom from fresh air. *(Enter Ant., Hero, Marg., Ther.)* Look, there's Antony. Hurra, for Antony !

All.—Hurra !

Ant.—   Thanks friends,
For such you must be to give this greeting
To one who has not earned it. You better
Save your lungs, for there are some coming soon
Who deserve your applause.

Tom.—If I had done what you have, I would knock him down, who would not greet me well.

Ant.—Here is the porch all fitted for our comfort.

Hero.—And a lovely view for quite a distance
Up and down.

Marg.—   That's why we gave
The invitation. 'Twer hardly worth one
From a lesser view.

Ant.—We have not long to place ourselves, so we
May as well use all the time. But where is
Leopole ?

Ther.— He had an errand to fulfil
But promised to be here ere now. Here he comes.
You go in the while, I'll wait for him.

Ant.—Another private interview, still you'll
Deny your sick.

Ther.—Well I'll not have your physician
For you grow worse.

Marg.—What you say Antony, seems but to feed her wit.
(Exit Ant., Hero, Marg. Enter Leo. Ther. helps them in.)

Leo. (aside)—Now to my fiendish work, for such it is,
To mention friendly things to Antony
While I think but of harming him, the which
I am sorry is necessary to
My ambitious desires. Why was I
Ever famous ? That now I must so envy
Antony to sustain myself and
In the guise of friendship play the villian.
Oh, dam this weakening. I'll not endure
Being common. *(Ther. comes to Leo.)*

Ther.— You are very punctual.

Leo.—There is a clock in every lover's mind,
That is regular through love, and he who
Is tardy in his love meetings, loves not.

Ther.—You talk of love to me I doubt you,
You know so many others.

Leo.— Were we not
So conspicuous here, I would prove my love.
If humbling myself to you would do it.

Ther.—You seem to cold and wise for a lover.

Leo.— These citizens, these slaves
Of love and passion, would mock at true love
Were they to see it. But tell me, have you
The tie you promised to procure ?

Ther.— Yes, here it is,
But I would like to know what value it has
To you.

Leo.— 'T was Antonys, he wore it as

A mascot, he claimed it had a charm, and
As I am supersticious, I value it.

Ther.—They must not know how you came by it.

Leo.—They never shall. (*Antony appears on porch.*)

Ant.— I know a stanza
That each of you could sing to the other
And save your wit, for 'tis just what you wish
To say : I love my love in the morning, I love,
(*Hero, Marg. come on the porch.*)
But come up they are approaching. (*Exit Leo, Theo.*)

Bill.—He is wide in the shoulders.

Tom.—Less than Antony and smaller legged.

Bill.—Use your eyes, use your eyes man, and see
That Leopole is larger every way
And better proportioned.

Tom.— Man you talk through drink.
'Tis plain to common sense, that Antony
Is best man, he conquered Leopole.
Could he if he were worse ?
(*Officer passes and places them in line.*)

Bill.—Yes when Leopold let him. There was naught
At stake. Leopole would wager
A dozen fortunes on another trial,
But Antony refuses for fear.

Tom.— He lost
his reputation that was worth a fortune.

Bill.—What is reputation ? wind, nothing else.

Tom.—'Tis on reputation most money 's made.

Bill.—Have your way to stop your crying.

Tom.— I'm not
crying and I wont be. But you know I'm right.

Bill.—Go sleep it off, your brain is muddy.

Tom.—No, my brain is not muddy.

Bill.—Go away. (*Pushes him.*)

Tom.—No, I'll not go.

Bill.—Go away I say, I'm through with you. (*Pushes him again.*)

Tom.—No, you can't push me. (*They fight, officer arrests them.*)

Bill.—'T was his fault.

Tom.—No, he began it by insulting me.

(*Exit officer, Bill, Tom prisoners.*)

Hero.— How brutal were
Those men, I should think, their bones are broken.

Ant.—They are intoxicated and cannot
Hurt each other. They will forget this, and
Be friends when they are sober.

Hero.—You seem well schooled as to the effect of drink.

Ant.—Oh well, a man needs not be a debauch
To know the effects of liquor, a few
Good sprees will teach him.

Hero.—I thought my Antony was temperate.

Ant.—I have been since I told you so, but I
Had sprees before then. (*Enter the porch Leo, Ther.*)

Leo. (*aside.*)—This cobble must I push off
While Charles is passing as though Antony
Maliciously had hurled it at him. I am
Not myself. I would do what 'ere is prompted.

Ant.—Oh, such a spectacle. Look! Look! He was wise
Who first suggested uniforms for soldiers,
For while formidable to the enemy
They inspire a friend. See how more imposing
Than the citizens, and yet they are but people.

Marg.—I think Antony chose wrong to become
An athlete.

Hero.—A soldier is so much abroad. (*Band passes.*)

Ant.— And this martial music,
Makes one almost wish for foes.

Leo. aside.—You need not wish for them,
Keep interested so 'twill make my task
More easy. (*A company passes.*)

Ant.—This is a brave company, Captain Beache's,
Look, that's he with the medals. They're for
His bravery, they rhyme to his courage,

The hottest fight is his delight.
His comrades seem to know naught but stories
Praising him.
But see, here comes Charles, how imposing grand.

Leo. aside.—My cue to be prepared.

Ant.—   There is a charm
In fame makes all curious to see him
They would pass a thousand times unnoticed
Were he unknown. (*Appear Char., Abr. on horseback.*)

Leo. aside.—   Be steady my hand
For if by accident I should down Charles,
I down myself. (*Ant. leans far over.*)

Ant.—Hurra for Charles. (*Leo. pushes cobble.*)

Char.—Treachery, traitors, a conspiracy, (*he unhorses himself*).
Soldiers seize him, surround the house, cut off
His escape. 'Twas Antony hurled this cobble
Towards our person; seize him he is a traitor,
Search the house for more, he shall be rewarded,
Who 'ere takes him or his accomplices,
For no doubt he is not alone in this.
How can we govern safely with enemies
So near in friendship to our person?

Ant.—What madcap spouting do you here to call me
Traitor, and offer honors to my captors? (*jumps down.*)
Here, win them yourself, for I did ever
Wish to help you to them. (*Exit above, Hero, Ther., Marg.*)

Char.—   Seize him, he is
Dangerous who so publicly offers harm.

Abr.—There must be some mistake, an accident.

Char.—An accident, to come so near my life?
No, 'tis a studied plot, I saw him hurl it.

Ant.—   You lie!
And know you do, but you're so used to that
You have them studied and they come easy,
But this is serious, I'll not deny
I caused that cobble to fall, but 'twas an accident.

Char.—You lie! I saw you hurl it!

Ant.— I'll crowd
That lie back in spite of your position. (*Ant. downs him.*)

Char.—Seize him men. (*Soldiers hold Ant.*)
(*Enter Hero, Marg., Ther., Leo.*

Hero.— My Antony, was it
Your accident caused this transformation
From blissful liberty to stern captivity?

Ant.— That's his excuse,
But I swear he has some deeper motive
That prompts him to it.

Hero to Char.—And do you for this wish him prisoner?

Char.—What more terrible crime could he commit,
Than attempt the lives of the duke's officers?

Hero.— 'Tis false,
I swear it! I have been his inmost friend
For many years and I know his mind,
And have oft heard him praise
Your qualities and ambition. He was
The first to applaud your every promotion,
Of all your friends he was most eager to hear from you,
And good news he would address as though
Your person with: Brave, Charles, with but a few
More strides we shall say Great Charles. 'Twas he
Suggested as my father knows, all these
New entertainments for to-day, and he
Worked for their completion so inceasingly,
There was no time for conspiring. And now
You call him your enemy and a traitor
For this small accident that only seemed to harm.

Char.—This is no woman's affair.

Hero.— I did not
Wish to settle it, but I told what I know.

Char.—It matters not what you do know, friendship
Must be forgot in dealing with traitors.

(*To Cap.*)—Captain, deal with him quickly and severely,
We'll rid ourselves of traitors. You have my orders.

Abr.— Stop, you have not mine,
And I am master yet. From noon my office
Will be yours, but till then I shall command.

Char.—There's no commanding in this case, there is
A special decree to hang all traitors.

Abr.—Yes, when it's proven they're traitors.

Char.—And is he not who came so near my life?

Abr.—It is not proven.

Char.—He shall be arrested and tried?

Abr.—That he shall.

Char.—Captain,
Take him to prison and have him doubly
Bound and guarded.

Abr.— Citizens,
As the gods with their disposing power,
Have thought best to place in Antony's lot
This accident by which his enemies
Do draw suspicion on him, he shall
For their satisfaction be tried just like
A criminal. So we must
Postpone our celebration, and once more
Do our office duties which we thought were through.

Char.—Away with him to prison.

(Exit Char., Leo. one side, the rest the other.)

(Scene closes.)

(Scene 2.)   *A Street.*

(Enter Citizens Meeting.)

1st Cit.—Hallo Jack! Where away so fast?

Jack.—I'm going to dress up and go to the trial.

1st Cit.—What trial is to you so interesting?

Jack.—You ask what trial? Why, where have you been man,
drunk or fishing?

1st Cit.—Neither, but what makes you so excited?

Jack.—And have you not heard that Bill and Tom are arrested, and Antony, the athlete, too ?

Cit.—Bill and Tom and Antony.   What's Antony done ?

Jack.- Attempt on the life of Charles.   While he was passing Antony's house, Antony from a porch hurled a cobble at him and most killed him.   They think it is some conspiracy and more are in it whom they must catch, but they will try Antony right off.

Cit.—Is Charles hurt much ?

Jack.—Just scraped his leg, he was on horseback.

Cit.-- Could'nt Antony escape ?

Jack.—He did'nt try.   He was on the porch and Charles was offering rewards to who would capture him, and he jumped down and says : ·'Take me yourself."

Cit.—The fool.   Got scared after he d done it, no doubt.

Jack.—No, no, he claimed 'twas an accident he could not help.

Cit. — The law won't excuse him from that.   Accidents don't count in law.   When I fell through Jerry's window 'twas an accident, but I had to pay.

2d Cit.—He's gone for if he monkeys with the law.

Jack.—Well, he's arrested, and I am going to see what they'll do with him.   Charles wanted the soldiers to take and hang him from where they were, but old Abe would'nt have it. He said he had to be tried first.

1st Cit.—Oh, he'll go free, I bet.   He goes with Abe's daughter, he's in the clique.   If it were any one of us, they'd a shot us on the spot.

Jack. — I don't think Antony's a traitor.   I think 'twas an accident.

2d Cit.—So do I, I don't think he's that kind.

1st Cit.—Why should he turn traitor ?   Sure not for gain, and I'd rather have his honors than Charles.

2d Cit.—And I.   But why are Bill and Tom in again ?   Fighting I suppose.

Jack.—They were arguing and neither would give the other the point and be laughed at, so they fought it out.

1st Cit.—Who whipped ?

Jack.—'Twas close, they're both game.

1st Cit.—Both brave men with lots of sand. You must knock out either to make him give in.

2d Cit.—I've seen both take hard trashings and not squeal.

Jack.—'Twas a pretty fight as far as it went, and if it had not been stopped, it'ld a been well worth seeing through. Tom gave Bill a nice uppercut.

2d Cit.—Who stopped them ?

Jack.—Oh, thick Dugan, and if I'ld a been either, I'ld a given him one would a done him good.

2d Cit.—One is all he'ld stand, he's a very coward, no more sand than a rabbit. He got a good punishment from me once before he was officer. He's no good.

Jack.—Well, I'm off, I want to see this trial. Coming ?

All.—Shure.

(*Scene closes.*)

(Scene 3.)   *Charles, Officers in Courthouse.*

(*Enter Char., Leo and guards.*)

Char.—   Go, guards,
Try and find accomplices in this plot,
Leave us, for I think we're safe within
These walls. (*Exit guards.*)
       Dam your clumsiness that almost
Made me cripple.

Leo.—   'Twas not intended I
Assure you. But then 'tis well, 'twill make our plot
More like a treacherous conspiracy
Against your person. .

Char.—   What! To cripple me
For evidence against my enemies ?
Hold you my word so light ? No, no, my word's
Enough. I, as their future judge must have
Some power, and I say : He is a traitor.

Leo.—Yes, but Abraham, the present judge
　　Will not believe it.　He has some power.

Char.—　　　　　　　He must believe it !
　　I'll not let that gray bearded fool best me.
　　Besides he can reckon the lasting of
　　His power in minutes, it is so short,
　　Then I will have full sway, and woe to him
　　Who interferes with or proposes aught
　　Against my wishes.

Leo.—　　　　　　　Yes, but Abe is still
　　In power and will be through this trial.

Char.—How can we prevent it?

Leo.—　　　　　　　Why, I will be
　　A doubtful witness, as though I knew not
　　How to think, neither favouring nor opposing
　　Antony.　One that has seen much and yet
　　Knows little, and I'll be as though unwilling
　　To disclose that little.　And then you make
　　The questioning of me very minute.
　　That way this trial will easily outlast
　　The remainder of his term.

Char.—　　　　　　　Good point,
　　You should have studied law.

Leo.—But I see they're coming, 'twer best we were
　　Not seen together in private.　I'll be
　　Away and you can learn their plans.

Char.—　　　　　　　Be where
　　I can find you.　(*Exit Leo.*)　Now to convince old Abe
　　There was a plot against me.　(*rubs his leg.*)
　　　　　　　I'ld much rather
　　This had not happened.　(*Enter Abr. and others.*)

Abr.—　　　　　　　Go find the officers
　　Of this court and summon them for speedy
　　Business. (*Exit Officers.*) (*To Char.*) A sad task you've
　　Made for me by accusing Antony of treason.

Char.—Sad indeed, sad to you and sad to me,
　　For who would have ever thought that treason

Lurked, where I looked for my warmest friendship,
That makes me sad.

Abr.—You lie, you cur, Antony's no traitor,
Nor he never bore a treacherous thought
Against you, nor he'ld never hear one spoke
Without through loyalty, he would proclaim
It's author. No, no, 'tis that empty hotbed
Of lies you call your brain, lied to your mind
That there was cause for jealousy, for there
Is nothing else to prompt this
Terrible accusation. But it is
Well you may be jealous of one you are,
So much inferior to. But until
You are king of all the earth, until your
Word alone is law, you'll not harm Antony
Unjustly.

Char.—When one has so plain to all beholders,
Come so near my life, is it then unjust
To accuse that one of treason ? I think
It is a loyal sacrifice when that one
Is so dear a friend.

Abr.—   You sacrifice
Your friendship, it must be very fickle,
I pity him whose livelihood depended
On it.

Char.—I want no more scolding. He's to
Be tried, then let him prove he s innocent. (*Exit Char.*)

Abr.—There's no treachery on record that has
A more contemptable object than your own,
That Antony is innocent, I would
Stake my life, my honor and my fortune
On it. I am so confident that had
He fled, I'ld stand his trial, if God above
Who knows his conscience, were to be judge.

(*Enter Officers of Court.*)

Fellow officers of this court, though we
Have named this day a holiday and set
It apart for celebration, we find

It necessary through an unforseen
Happening to retract our edict and
Make this one of our busiest days, for
Great Antony, whom you all know, is accused
Of treason gainst Charles, whom we were to
Install in our stead. So you all prepare
Yourselves with your utmost speed. (*Exit Officers.*)
Oh God in heaven, look down upon thy
Noble Antony and aid him in thy
Mysterious way, for well thou knowest
He is an innocent victim of proud
Charles' spite. (*Exit Abr., enter Char., Leo.*)

Leo.—A well laid plot, your quite an architect.

Char.—And if, like a builder, you follow my
Plans, you'll build the evidence that will crush
Antony, and you'll build yourself once more
To fame and fortune.

Leo.—   I am to far gone
In this to flinch at anything. But that tie,
You have no use for it now. (*Shows the tie.*)

Char.—   Shure I have (*takes the tie*)
I thought at first that this should bring me my
Revenge, but for that we've other means, so
With this I'll worry him and feed my spite.
Go you to him, wear this, wear it where he'll
See it, as though by accident, wear it
Loosely as though it had no value, and,
Should he question you, why invent some lie,
As, some friend of yours took it from his mistresses
Leg. Mention a struggle for it and how
Some oath went with her wearing it. Why I
Could coin lies forever with this start, and
Each would be as a knife to him. (*Exit Leo.*)
                           All goes well,
All seem to be in sympathy with me
And aiding me to my revenge. I never
Ment to be so hard on Antony, but
This chance offered to me when I was hot

With rage at Hero's refusal, seemed like
The only means to sooth me, and I have
Ventured till there is so retiring.   (*Enter Hero.*)
Ah Hero, you are indeed a welcome
Sight to me in my misfortune.

Hero.—   I am not here
To please you, but to sue to you, my lord.

Char.—I am not your lord. Be more intimate Hero.

Hero.—You hold Antony's liberty in your
Power, so you are his lord, and his lord
Is mine. You can proclaim him innocent
And set him free, 'tis for that I came to sue.

Char.—Hero, believe me, Antony's transgression
Wounds me as much as you, but we must be
Severe with traitors to discourage them.

Hero.—Antony's no traitor as you know well.
,You dare speak of him but not to him as such.

Char.—Why bother ourselves of him, you know a
Traitors doom is death. He was much to you
But soon shall be no more, then may I sue
In your affections to take his place ?

Hero.—Think you I would encourage a man who
Downed my Antony ? No! If Antony
Dies, why so do I to all the world. I
Would live and die a dry old spinster with
No occupation but training flowers
For his monument. But Charles, I came to
Beg of you to retract your charge and set
My Antony free.

Char.—   There's but one way to
Set him free, and that's at your disposal.

Hero.—And how is that ?

Char.—   Give your consent to be
My wife and Antony shall live.

Hero.—If I wished to become your wife I would
Not sue for Antony's freedom, for I
Did not think my chance with you was doubtful.

Char.—For your consent to marry me, and for
    Nothing else will I aid this traitor to
    His liberty.

Hero.—Then give me time to bring this proposition
    To him. If he consents, why so do I.
    I will sacrifice myself for him. (*Exit Hero.*)

Char.—I never thought I would have her so soon
    In supplication t'wards me, nor did she,
    When she this morning so proudly spurned me.
    But nor his consent nor your consent
    Can make me aid to save him now, for then
    I'ld be suspected. (*Enter Alice.*)

Alice.—I like the way you kept me prisoner.

Char.—Well, no doubt it tamed you.

Alice.—Oh no, it has made me wild and I've heard
    What you have done and what else you intend.
    But I will stop you by telling what I
    Overheard this morning. That will be my
    Revenge, and perhaps it will tame you. I
    Thought to find a lady here and tell her
    What I heard but now that she is gone I'll
    Go tell Antony, it might be useful
    To him.

Char.—   No, no. Don't go to him!

Alice.—   Oh, but
    I will, for what I know is a burden
    On my mind, and I wish to be relieved. (*Approach Abr.*)

Char.—You shall not go.

Alice.—But I'm going. (*Starts out.*)

Char.—I say you won't go, and you won't. (*Stops her.*)

Alice.—Let me go. Help! (*Abr. seperates them.*)

Abr.—The lady wishes to go. (*to Alice*) Go!
                   (*Exit Alice.*)

                     (*Scene closes.*)

Act. III. *A Prison Cell and Courtyard.*

(Antony discovered bound.)

Ant.—Heaven grant me depth of reason to clear
The mystery which surrounds my being here,
There never happened, that I remember
T'wix Charles and I, aught that could gall him thus
To disgrace me for revenge. Could my fame
Have made him wish to crush me, and could that
Star which rules my destiny, have caused that
Cobble to fall for his opportunity ?
No, our professions are so different,
They never could cause jealousy.   Can it
Be writ in my destiny, that this accident
Should seem like treachery to Charles ? No, no,
There's something gall's him, that he gave so cold
A greeting for a so long seperated
Friend. I hope my being Hero's choice is
No motive for his hateing me, but
Who knows ? Rejected lovers have become
So desperate, no punishment had terrors
For them. If I thought she favored him, but
Clung to me for her promises sake I
Willingly would forget her for him, but
If by cheat he tried to part us he would
Have to tear me from her each joint singly.

(Enter the yard Wiggins and Assistants.)

Wig.—Come, Swipes, there's not much time. We may use this
grave to-day. You dig here.

Swi.—Now why should I dig ? They won't bury him in the
court yard. 'Twill be unnecessary work on me and I think
I do enough for my pay.

Wig.—You've done nothing but run for grog to-day.

Swi. —There was nothing else to do, and there is no need of
looking for unnecessary work.

Wig.—If he is to be shot we'll bury him here. So you dig a
grave.

Swi.—I know it will be unnecessary work on me and then filling
it up again, more unnecessary work.

Wig.—It must be done, so dig away.

Swi.—This way or that ?

Wig.—Length ways of course.

Swi.—How long ?

Wig.—Well, he's tall, make it twice your shovel.
And you joiners, here's your timbers, build a gallows.
(*they go to work.*)   Now I've
Known Antony from boyhood until now,
And a wilder boy there never was.
Well liked and honest outside of what boy's
Motto teaches; that, stolen fruit is sweetest;
He was the last man I thought to have as
Prisioner.   (*Joiners hammer, Antony starts.*)

Ant.—What fickle fear this forced confinement gives.
I start like one with a guilty conscience.
(*Wig. knocking*)   Hallo Antony.

Ant.—Hallo you.

Wig.—May I come in ?

Ant.—If I could let you in I'ld not be here myself.
                   (*Enter Wig., Joiners hammer.*)

Ant.—What hammering is that, it quite unnerves me,
But I know not why.

Wig.—'Tis a gallows they are building.

Ant.—For who ?

Wig.—Perhaps for you.

Ant.—So serious.   No, no.   He may take
My honor but he cannot wish my life.

Wig.—I have often wished to wring your neck
When you were at my apples, but I never thought
I'ld have to do it.

Ant.—   You never shall,
Not for my crimes, for were they all summed up,
There would be but a father's whipping due.
'Tis not for being a criminal that I

Am here, but for being an impediment
Somehow to the desires of Charles, but I
Know not whether it be in honor or
In love.

Wig.— Antony,
You've oft made me so desperate mad, I've
Almost broke my teeth in grinding them and
Cursing you in anger. Yet I believe
You innocent in this. I believe you'ld
Take a farm for deviltry, but would not
Steal an apple for it's value. (*Hero, Marg. enter yard.*)

Marg.—Charles made this proposition ? .

Hero.—Yes.

Marg.—What will you do ?

Hero.— Just what my Antony
Bids me do. If he will have his freedom,
I'll be the ransom, if not I'll die
With him, I'll not have Antony either
Way, so there's no choice but death, for to
Live without him I will not. What's this, a
Gallows and a grave ? They must be for
Antony.

Marg.—I'll ask him. (*to Swipes.*)
May I ask you what you are doing ?

Swi.—Certainly.

Marg.—Well, what are you doing ?

Swi.—Unnecessary work.

Marg.—What is it to be ?

Swi.—A grave.

Marg.—For whom ?

Swi.—For Wiggins, the jailor.

Marg.—Is he dead ?

Swi.—No.

Marg.—Then why are you digging a grave for him ?

Swi.—'Tis for him, but 'tis not his. He has a prisioner they
will either hang or shoot. If they shoot him he gets buried
here, so I must dig the prisioners grave for Wiggins. He's
the jailor.

Marg.—Whose grave is it to be ?

Swi.—A genuine villian's, I assure you. One who has often
plagued me most to death. I would be glad they sentenced
him only it makes for me unnecessary work.

Marg.—Who is the villain ?

Swi.—One Antony, and I have oft wished him harm,
I'm happy if they shoot him.

Hero.—He is not sentenced yet so don't you be
Elated fool. And Margaret, until
He is we will not mourn but try to aid him.

Wig.—I will believe you innocent no matter what the sentence
but I cannot aid you for I am but hired. Good by.
                          (*Wig. comes out of cell.*)

Ant.—Good by Wiggins, and forget my misdemeanor.

Hero.—This must be the jailor. I'll ask him.
    (*to Wig.*) Are you the jailor, sir ?

Wig.—Yes, Miss.

Hero.—Have you the care of Antony ?

Wig.—Yes, Miss.

Hero.—May we see him ?

Wig.—If he will have it certainly. He is in there.

Marg.—I am his sister.

Wig.—Then I guess he won't refuse to see you.
This way, but I must lock you in with him.

Hero.—Possession is nine points of the law. Then
Charles with this much start could easily find
Means to hold us there, but as long as he
Holds Antony I wish to be held to. (*they enter.*)

Ant.—You are two more that I'll swear believe me
Innocent.

Hero.—Oh Antony, what hellish fate is this
Comes so abrupt into our happiness ?

Ant.—I know not Hero, unless it is our fate.
I can think of nothing that could be his
Motive for wishing me removed, and I'll
Swear he knows as well as God above that
I'm no traitor, or ever saught his life.
But how goes the cry among the citizens
And my friends ? Do they believe me guilty ?

Marg.—All that I have heard do sympathize
With you, not that they think you guilty, but
For being unjustly charged with treason.

Ant.—What's being done towards my case ?

Marg.—They are making all preparations for a
Speedy trial ere Charles term begins.

Hero.—I've been to Charles to know his mind.

Ant.—What said he ?

Hero.—He would have me think that your transgression
As he called it, gave him much pain.

Ant.—Then he firmly intends to convict me ?

Hero.—No, he made a proposition for your life.

Ant.—How liberal. Until now I never
Knew he had the power to hang or shoot
A man, or let him live just to his liking,
But what's his proposition ? I will listen
How 'ere absurd.

Hero.—He says on this condition only will he
Retract his charge. That I will marry him.

Ant.—So that's the cause of his dislike for me.
And had he the nerve for this proposal ?
He must think me a degraded plebian
Who loves himself alone. No, no, Hero,
I love my wife and would sooner die than
She should be sacrificed to him.
A miserable measily coward
And no one else would
Try to benefit himself in this way.
It cannot be that you encouraged him.

Hero.—I did not encourage him, I merely

Listened, thinking only of doing what
I could for you. And when he finished I
Came here in all haste for your opinion.

Ant.—You should know me better than to think me
Of such fickle mettle. I'ld never approve
Of sacrificing you to save myself.

Hero.—Think Antony, he'll murder you if I refuse.

Ant.—No, no, my Hero. He has not so much
Power. He has made a charge of treason
Against me, and I must stand a trial.
But he must prove it ere he can harm me,
So I fear him not, no more than that he
Can make much trouble for me if he chooses.

(*Leo. enter court yard.*)

Leo.— Now I am to do
More dirty work. I am but Charles tool.
Oh courage, this is no time to falter,
I have been a fickle simpleton ever since
I entered this plot against Antony.
One thought makes me sorry and repenting
And the next one gives me courage. I hope
He will see this tie and then again I
Hope he wont for fear of what he'll say.

Hero.—I will go to him once more, and see if I
Can make him sorry for what he's done.

Ant.—No, no, your supplication will but make him prouder.

Hero.—I'll not feel satisfied till I've done all I can.

Leo.—Jailor, may I see Antony ?

Wig.—He has company now. (*Hero knocks.*)
But I guess they wish to leave, (*opens the door.*)

Marg.—You need not be lonesome for here comes
Leopole, so I'll go away with Hero. (*Exit Hero, Marg.*)

Leo.—Antony, accept my sympathy,
For a case like yours I never heard of.

Ant.—Thanks, Leopole, for I am anxious that my friends
Should think me innocent. But Leopole,

Did you take note of how that cobble fell ?
I was so interested I did not.

Leo.—   I'm sure I did not, for I
Was interested too. You did lean forward though.

Ant.—   I was much interested,
And so I think it happened, but it pains
Me most that he I've done so much for, was
So easily provoked to wish me harmed,
For had he but common sense, he must know
It was an accident.

Leo.—   Perhaps there is
Some rivalry between you.

Ant.—   So it seems,
For he now wishes Hero's hand in marriage.

Leo.—He knows not his own mind for within this hour
He told me he would never marry, as
He had the using of more women now
Than he could tend to and stay healthy.

Ant.—Were you with him ?

Leo.—I went to pump him, for why he charged you
With conspiracy. But he would not talk
Of that, he seemed more interested in
Some foolish woman as he called her, who
Loved him unreasonably.

Ant.—   Would he
Not mention what caused his sudden hate for me ?

Leo.—No. As often as I broached your case, he would start off
about this woman. Says he : She's a maid, mind you, about
to be married to another, but she so loves me, she sought
my aid to rid herself of this other, whom she cared not for.

Ant.—Would he not say if it was not impulse made him accuse
me ?

Leo.—I tried him every way but 'twas no use,
He would talk of nothing else but this maid. Why,
Says he : She is so conquered by my charms,
She will discard her promised husband,
Though not point blanc, through modesty, so she

Brought a plot to him, to lure her lover
From the scent.

Ant.—   And is he so unconcerned
About a life which almost depends on him?

Leo.—He said this plot was to remove
Forever this prospecting husband
As an impediment. And then he laughed.

Ant.—Who was this maid? and who her promised husband?

Leo.—He would not say. It seemed to please him most
To keep that secret. He claimed I know her well
But could never guess.
Said how she loved him ere he went away
But loved him more on his return.
He thought his station made the extra love,
That's why he cared so little for her.

Ant.—And how came he to her?

Leo.   She came to him,
And was overcome embracing him when
Her lovers sister appeared and stopped the fun.
But he has seen her since and she's now stale.
She had her lovers necktie as a garter.
Tied there with an oath, this he removed
And cared so little for it, he threw it at me.
And I thought so well of it that I do wear it.

          (Ant. sees it and starts.)

Ant.—Who was she, say you?

Leo.—I know not, but no doubt some common strumpet.

Ant.—   You lie!
She who wore that tie was no such thing nor
Ever stayed with Charles. 'Tis another of
His dirty plots to sully her pure name,
He's not content with ruining mine.

Leo.—Do you know her?

Ant.—No, no, no. But what he's done to me makes
This opinion of him. No doubt 'tis true
For there are many

That greatness will enamor.   But you say,
She brought some plot which would remove her husband?

Leo.—So he told me but he'ld not mention what it was.

Ant.—And she was stale to him?

Leo.—Yes, Antony.   But why this agitation?

Ant.—Oh nothing.   Leopole, my being prisioner
Has quite unnerved me, I am not fit
To entertain you, Leopole, leave me
As a friend.   (*Leo. knocks.*)

Leo.— I will Antony, and will do my best
To appease your prosecutor.   (*Wig. unlocks.*)

Leo.—   Good by, Antony.

Ant.—Good by.   (*Exit Leo. to court yard.*)

Leo.—That must have hurt.   'Twill cause
This mental agony which has nothing
Visable for arrousing sympathy,
Like the bleeding of some painless cut which
Would bring tears and sighs and gentleness from all.   (*Exit.*)

Ant.—Hero Charles'es stale and plotting against
Her lover, why that is me.   No, I'll not
Believe it.   But he had my tie and she
Said, if any man could show me that, she'ld
Not deny he has seduced her.   What brought
Those thoughts to her?   She plotted to rid herself
Of her intended husband.   Why, she was
On the porch, could she have pushed that cobble?
No, no.   She would not, yet it appears I
Did not for I felt no jar which I would have
Had my weight been on it.   She did admit
She came from him to me and would return
To him.   But then I'll not believe it.   Hero
Is true to me.   He said her lover's sister
Caught her embraceing him.
Why that is Margaret, I'll be convinced.   (*Calls Wig.*)
(*Enter Wig.*)

Ant.—Is Margaret about?

Wig.— Yes, she's at the gate.

Ant.—Bring her to me. (*Exit Wig.*)
Now she can prove if Hero is false to me,
She will not lie. (*Enter Marg.*)

Ant.—When did you first see Charles since his return?

Marg.—Why this morning, when we had left you to
Your lovemaking for a while, I returned
To tell you something,
Charles must have come just ere I entered, for
Hero was just greeting him, and as I
Am not familiar with him, I retired
Ere they had seen me.

Ant.—Were they familiar?

Marg.—Why sure they were. Why not? They are old friends,
Why they embraced like lovers.

Ant.—What's that, you too against me? Have I
No friends on earth? No, no, Margaret, I
Believe you, but Hero is false to me.
She is Charles'es mistress,
'Twas she who plotted for my life, I am
An obstacle to her enjoying him,
She s with her lover now, I'll soon be there
Myself and to catch them while embraceing
Will be much more convincing proof.
                    (*tugs at his bonds.*)
                        Break! break!
Don't think you can withstand a desperate
Athlete's strength. (*breaks away.*)

Marg.—Why Antony, what do you mean?

Ant.—Away! Don't bother me now,
I'm not accountable for my deeds.

            (*breaks the door, Wig. tries to stop him.*)

Ant.—Out of my way, out of my way!

        (*Knocks Wig. and Assitants down and exit.*)

            (*Scene closes.*)

(Scene 2.) *A Street.*

(*Citizens discovered.*)

1st Cit.—Think you they will punish Antony with his life ?

2d Cit.—Shure. 'Tis evident he is a traitor, and they either hang or shoot them. But he went so open about it and missed.

1st Cit.—The fool, with the risk he ran he should have made it more shure.

2d Cit.—Had he killed Charles he would not suffer more.

1st Cit.—And yet they call him so great.

2d Cit.—He is good at wrestling.

1st Cit.—He has no head, so he proved to-day, and it takes a head to wrestle. I always did think Leopole gave him that last match.

2d Cit.—Yes, I guess you're right. Well, if they convict him Leopole will again be champion.

1st Cit.—Yes, and I would sooner see him too.

2d Cit.—And if this ain't him, I don't know him. Speak of any one but the devil and they'll appear. Did you ever know that proverb to fail ? I did'nt.

1st Cit.—Nor I either. (*Enter Leo.,* *they salute him.*)
Hurra for Leopole ! Hurra !

Leo.—How do you do, gentlemen ? Happy days. (*Exit Cit.*)
Figuring on Antony's
Execution they but surmise I'll rise
And already greet my fortune.
They little know the sneaky way I use
To gain that fortune, but that matters not,
They would not greet me for my morals. I
Am sorry I ever entered this plot
With Charles, but he will pay me for my share
I'll warrant, and that before it is too late.

(*Exit Leo., enter Citizens.*)

1st Cit.—You never saw Leopole ? I thought everybody knew him. There he goes, that's him.

3d Cit.—-A noble man, fine proportioned.

2d Cit.—And right worthy of holding the championship.

1st Cit.—There is none can down him.

2d Cit.—He's a good spender, I often drank on him.

3d Cit.—Where does he be often ?

1st Cit.—Nowhere in particular, everywhere or anywhere, just as it happens.

2d Cit.—What is this crowd coming ?

1st Cit.—They're chasing some one.

3d Cit.—Who can it be ?

2d Cit.—A madman.

1st Cit.—Ain't that Antony ?

2d Cit.—As I live it is.   He has escaped.

1st Cit.—They're trying to stop him.

3d Cit.—Let's help them.

2d Cit.—I'll not, he looks desperate.

1st Cit.—Nor I.   He has a lions strength.   (*Enter Ant.*)

Ant.—Make way there, I'll kill the first man hinders me.

* (*Rushes across the stage, knocks citizens down and exit.*)

(*Scene closes.*)

(Scene 3.)   *Charles Office.*

(*Enter Hero, Alice following.*)

Alice.—I had quite a race to overtake you,
  So now I hope you'll listen to me.

Hero.—Why shure I will listen, but
  I have important business bids me haste.

Alice.—I doubt not but what I have to say
  Concerns your business.   'Tis of Antony
  I would speak.

Hero.—What do you know of him ?

Alice.—That his arrest was plotted for by those
  He thought were his best friends.

Hero.—How plotted for ?

Alice.—Charles has some dislike for him, and he holds

What once were Leopole's honors, so they
Plotted for his ruin.

Hero.—How do you know all this ?

Alice.—I overheard them propose an accident
From the porch as Charles would pass.

Hero,—You mean the falling of that cobble
Was prearranged by Charles and Leopole ?

Alice.—I do, and that Leopole pushed it purposely
And not Antony by accident as you think.

Hero.—If what you say be true 'twill recreate
My hopes for future happiness, which I
Thought gone forever. But Leopole is
Antony's friend.

Alice.—   He but seems so. He was
Mine once too. I tell you I did hear him
Rail on fortune and on Antony for
Robbing him of it, and because he came
And went unnoticed, while Antony's
Every move and look would bring forth cheers.
Then he railed on me and cursed me so, I
Swore revenge, and my chance soon came, for Charles
Approached and told him of his grudge and how
By downing Antony.he'ld be revenged
And Leopole would be again in favour.

Hero.—And would you swear to this before them ?

Alice.—Yes, and before God Almighty.

Hero.—Then if Charles is to be found I'll
Bring him here and Antony will be free.
                    (*Exit Hero, enter Charles.*)

Alice.—Now you important one, we'll see who'll
Get the worst of this morning's quarrel.

Char.—Why, what do you mean ?

Alice.—What, why that she knows all that went between
You and Leopole this morning.

Char.—You told her of that plot ?

Alice.—Cert, and I'm going to swear to it at
The trial, if there is one.

Char.— You degraded wretch.
How far will your word go aside of ours ?

Alice.—I don't know or care. They may not believe me,
But I'll get them thinking.

Char.—If you don't leave this town and in a hurry,
I'll lock you up for what you are, not fit
To mingle with respectable people.

Alice.—Oh what I know does not amount to anything, yet you
wish me to leave town. Guess not. I would sooner stay
and bother you. And as for your having me arrested, ha !
I am in the business to long to think you can do it.

Char.—Where is she going ?

Alice.—To look for you and make you come down from your
high perch.

Char.—You've ruined me.

Alice.—I hope so, but I never thought I was so wise. (*knocking.*)

Char.—Will you step in this room until I find out what is
wanted ?

Alice.—And have you lock me in ? Oh no !

Char.—Then here into the hall, but don't leave for I have some
business with you. (*Exit Alice.*)

Char.—Come in. (*enter Officers.*) What's wanted ?

Offic.— I have a summons for you to appear at the trial of
Antony.

Char.—I will not fail to be there. (*Exit Officers, enter Leo.*)
You never arrived at a more fortunate time.

Leo.—What's up.

Char.—We're lost, unless by stratagem or
By some precious gem you can win Alice
To our favour. She has told Hero all
She overheard this morning.

Leo.—What ! I'll tear her heart out.

Char.—No, no, I have a better plan. She is
In love with you, make her think you return it.

Leo.—But I turned her from me this morning.

Char.— Give some excuse for that, as,
You were indisposed or so, and give her
All the gold she wants, I know she'll yield.

Leo.—Where is she ?

Char. — In the hall. Now you retire and when she gets here,
you happen in accidently as though you'ld not seen me, be
very affectionate. (*Exit Leo.*)

Char.—(*Opening the door.*) 'Tis now to late to refuse a risk on
an obstacle. (*Enter Alice.*) Important business has come
before me, which I must attend to immediately, you wait
here, I'll not be long and I must see you. (*Exit Char.*)

Alice.—I never thought I would be so lucky as to hold secrets
valuable to rich men. (*Enter Leo.*)

Leo.— Well, well, Alice,
You're looking splendid, charming enough
To tempt the coldest flesh. It seems an age
Of seperation I've been through, but we'll
Soon be again with fortune, and able
To revel to our heart's content.

Alice.—Who do you mean by we ?

Leo.—Why, you and I, of course. You're not surprised
I hope, that I know of your hankering
For sport ? I guess you've not reformed.

Atice.—Do you put this friendship on to mock me ?

Leo.— Come, come, Alice,
We've had too many rackets together
To act like moralists.

Alice.—I don't deny my business, but do you
Know that I squealed what I o'erheard this morning ?

Leo.—No ! To who ?

Alice.—To Hero.

Leo.—That will ruin all our sport. Why did you ?

Alice.—You used me rough this morning.

Leo.— And did you mind that ?
Have you never felt as though you hated
Yourself ? That's the way I felt this morning,

I did not know what I was saying. We've
Got to fix this some way or loose our sport,
For with Antony away I am the hero,
And you know me when I have money.
How did you fix it with Hero ?

Alice.—I told her all I heard and she wants to
Have me to swear to it at the trial.

Leo.—　　　　　　　　You go to the trial
And deny it all, deny you ever
Spoke to her. You will never be sorry.
Here's money for you to spend. See, I am
But on the way to fortune and I have
Money, I will have much more if you'll but
Help me to it. Will you deny all you
Told her for me ?

Alice.—I will deny I ever saw her on a bed of bibles.

Leo.—Good ! 'Tis not best we were seen together until all is
over, they might suspect.

Alice.—I'll go invest this money in silk stockings.

Leo.—Well, good by, until this is over, then we will swim in
wine.

Alice.—Adieu. (*Exit Alice.*)

Leo.—More dirty work, but that was easy.
I say Charles. (*Enter Char.*)

Char.—Well, how is she ?

Leo.—Blot her out as an obstacle.

Char.—How did you do it ?

Leo.—With little gold and big promises. But there is no time
to spare, I must see the prosecutor and buy him to lengthen
out this trial. (*Exit Leo.*)

Char.—'Tis not long till Antony will be no more,
Then I shall have proud Hero at my feet. (*Enter Hero.*)

Hero.—　　　　　　　Prepare yourself
For a mighty transformation. When last
We met I was at your command, now bow
Yourself in supplication.

Char.—This is indeed a transformation, but
Why should I bow. I am no miscreant.

Hero.—No, but a conspirator.

Char.—Why, how is that?

Hero.—   One who o'erheard you
Plotting to down Antony has told me all.

Char.—How absurd, that I should plot against one
Who awaits a death sentence.

Hero.—That death sentence
When I have told them all I know, will be yours.

Char.—Come, tell me all I am interested.

Hero.—Leopole and yourself this morning did conspire
To push that cobble from the porch, and then
Charge Antony with treason. You see I
Know it all and want you to settle
Antony's freedom. (*Appear Ant.*)

Char.—Go away, you rave. I hope your interlect
Is not impaired by love.

Hero.—I do love, I admit.

Ant. aside.—Too true, she does love him and I've been duped,
'Tis from her own lips.

Hero.—But think well before it is too late, think
Of the disgrace 'twill cause you.

Ant. aside.—She's stale to him and he'll not marry her.

Hero.—The dishonor to your name, to be arrested,
And have me prove you guilty.

Char.—Have me arrested, if you will, tell them all you know,
and see if a strumpet's word will outweigh mine. Leave
me, I have no use for you.

    (*Antony comes forward.*)   (*Appear jailor and guards.*)

Ant.—And little do I blame you Charles, for this
Discarding of a strumpet.

Hero.—My Antony, and free. (*goes to him, he pushes her away.*)

Ant.—   Yes,
Free from my prison bonds, and free from you,

Thank heaven.   By your plot for my disposal
You thought to ruin me, but you made me,
For far better is an honorable death,
Than life that's linked to your dishonor.

Hero.—What does my Antony mean ?

Ant.—You'll still use your dissembling gift, and play
The innocent.   T'wer better you were quiet,
And not add lies to your dishonor.

Hero.—As my Antony wishes.

Ant.—No, no, not yours, just as you wished it, and
Happy I to know 'tis so.   And may you
Have success in those desires in which I
Hindered you.   Come, officers, bring me back,
I will stand a trial, yes, and if sentenced
Die happy after what I have escaped.

(Guards take Antony.)

(Curtain.)

Act. IV. *Scene, Court Room.*

(*Enter Leo. and Prosecutor.*)

Leo.—You see, Antony will be tried this morning while Abraham is still in office, and he being interested in Antony, who is his daughter's intended husband, will hurry things through before Charleses term begins. Now what I want is, for you to do what you can to draw this trial into Charles'es term.

Pros.—No doubt something will turn up through which I can gain a stay for you.

Leo.—You being acquainted with the way of law would see a chance where others would'nt.

Pros.—True, and for our friendship's sake, I will use it to your advantage, though I have nothing against this Antony.

Leo.—That's what I want. Now come, we will drink together for luck. (*Exit both, enter Hero.*)

Hero.—Am I the first one here? Well, I should be,
For I am more interested than all others. (*kneels.*)
Heaven look with thy allseeing eye upon
The unjust misery thy righteous subject
Suffers, and with thy impartial mind convict
The true transgressor. Give thy judgement to
Thy officers below that they may punish
The guilty. (*rises.*)
Was ever woman in my plight? No, no,
Antony was not himself when he did spurn me.
An unjust imprisonment and charged with
Treachery by those he has considered
His dearest friends is enough to upset
The strongest mind. I have excused what he
Has done no matter what the source, and I
Will prove that I love him, though he would hate
My corpse. Here will I await what is to come.

(*Hero sits down, enter court officers, citizens, Char., Leo.*)

Hero.—You are well met though not by accident
For villians seek their kind for company.

Char. —I wish you knew the truth and had no faith
   In what you heard, then would you know us as friends-

Hero. —I sought no conversation with you, I
   Intended to insult you, but you are
   So hardened that I cannot.

Char. —We will leave you until you are convinced,
   We wish you well. (*They leave her.*)

Hero. —   Heaven only knows
   Its object in distributing such natures
   Here amongst us. Wickedness on earth
   Must be decreed by heaven, or else
   Such minds would not exist. But,
   Where can this woman stay ?

             (*Enter officers with Tom and Bill.*)

Tom. —Now to give the price of half a dozen good sprees to en-
   rich a rich city.

Bill. —I'm sorrier than you are, for its all your fault.

Tom. —Because I tried to stop you from making an ass of me its
   my fault. I'ld sooner be arrested, than showed up like
   that. (*Enter Antony guarded.*)

Bill. —Hallo ! What's he done ?

Tom. —He's not been fighting I'll warrant. for no one would
   tackle him. (*As Antony passes Hero she comes to him.*)

Hero. —Antony, do you not know me ?

Ant. —Take this woman from me or else release me
   That I may protect myself. (*Guards push her away, she
                    weeps, enter Marg.*)

Marg. to Hero. —Why not practice what you preach ?
   He is not sentenced yet and until he is
   We will not mourn.

Hero. —   He's worse than sentenced, he's mad.

Marg. —So I thought when I last saw him, as
   He charged me with conspiring for his life,
   Then forgave me, claimed you were false, and
   Plotting to dispose of him, then broke his bonds
   Rushed through the court yard, passed the guards, and

Until now I have not seen him. I
Will go speak to him.

Hero.—I doubt he will know you, he did not me.
And my presence seems to aggrivate him.

Marg.—Perhaps 'tis best I keep away.

Hero.—   Come with me.
They are not ready, and I will tell you
Of the plot makes Antony prisoner.
I heard it from a friend, and she must be found
As our main witness. (*Exit Hero and Marg.*)

Leo.—Can Hero have already told him what she heard ?

Char.—   Why no,
He would not listen to her when they met.
About the necktie and what else he heard
From you worked to perfection. Now if Alice
Will keep her word he will not know until
It is too late.

Leo.—She would do twice as much to win my smiles
If I'll but give them. I will go sympathize
With Antony. (*Goes over to Antony.*)
                    Antony, I can bring
But little consolation to you.

Ant.—Leopole, old friend, I don't want any,
The news you brought me in my cell
Was sufficient. You little knew how I
Was connected with that story, or perhaps
You did, but respecting my dejection,
Would not be bold by bringing more, but as
A friend gave me a clue to proofs. Was it
Not so, Leopole ? You're silent to respect
My feelings, and Leopole, twice dear you
Make your friendship by it. Through your clue I
Am convinced my love was trifling with me,
And now I welcome death as much as ever
I cared to live.

Leo.—   Antony, stop or I
Will wish for death myself.

Ant.—   No, no, you live,
Live and be famous, live and be honored
As an athlete, for the people must have one
For their amusement and their idol, and
Who is there but you that is worthy and
Entitled to their praise ? And Leopolo,
All the medals and trophys I have won
I've willed to you, they with my titles, when
I am dead are yours with my best wishes
That you honor them, and there is no one
More confident than I am that you will.

*Leo.—*Antony, you do not know me or you
Would not say this, you'ld sooner curse me, if
You knew my mind.

Ant.—   All ill feelings that have grown
From my victory over you, I do forgive,
For human nature makes us all jealous
Of our fame. (*Enter Abr., takes judge's seat.*)

Leo.—   The court is about to open,
I will leave you, and let heaven guide
Our future for the best. (*Leaves Antony.*)

*Sheriff.—*Oh yes, oh yes, this court is now opened. (*etc.*)

Abr.—   Fellow officers,
Though we had suspended business for this day,
Set it apart for holiday and rejoicing
As is a custom,
An unforseen accident has compelled us
To convene and give speedy redress to
An offended citizen. We will hear
Antony's case.

*Pros.—*Your Honor, the cases of Tom Sawyer and Bill Johnson
are first on the docket.

*Abr.—*This court convened to-day especially for Antony's case.

*Pros.—*There is no law that specifies certain prisoners shall be
favoured either for relationship to its servants or for their
social worth. (*reads*) Tom Sawyer and Bill Johnson,
breach of the peace.

Abr.— 'Tis not
His relationship to the officers
Of this court, nor his social standing makes
His case special, but the seriousness
Of the charge.

Pros.—All crimes are serious, and he must await his turn,
(*reads*) Tom Sawyer and Bill Johnson, breach of the peace.
(*They are brought forward.*)

Tom to Bill.—It's your fault we're in this pickle.

Pros.—You are charged with breach of the peace. To this
Charge what is your plea, guilty or not guilty ?

Tom.—You see Bill there, was not good humored.

Pros.—Are you guilty or not guilty ?

Tom.—He buckeled me and I resisted.

Pros.—I did not ask to hear your case. Are you
guilty or not guilty ?

Tom.—Well, we faught. If you call that
guilty, I am.

Pros. to Bill.—You are charged with breach of the
peace. To this charge what is your plea,
guilty or not guilty ?

Bill.—The same as him. If he's guilty, I am,
I won't squeal and try to put it all on to him,
I'll take my medicine like a man.

Abr.—This day being a holiday we will excuse
Your slight offense. You are discharged.

(*Tom and Bill start out.*)

Bill.—That's luck. If they had sent us up for thirty days, how
could .we have stood it without a drink ? I am as dry as
though I had lived on herring for a week. Let's hurry to
a saloon.

Tom. — We will go drown our happiness as some would
drown their sorrow. (*Exit both.*)

Abr.—Any more ahead of Antony ?

Pros.—Next comes Antony. (*He is brought forward.*)
You are charged with treason and attempt on the life of

Charles, one of the duke's officers.   To this charge what is
your plea, guilty or not guilty ?

Ant.—Not guilty.

Pros.—We will hear Charles.

Char.—What I have to say you all know well, that
While passing with the parade, where he was stationed,
A large cobble hurled with murderous intent,
Just missed its mission and scraped my knee, and
'Twas Antony that threw it.

Pros.—What have you to say to that ?

Char.—Such an accident happened.

Char.—   'Twas no accident.
He had some treacherous design
No doubt against this government.

Pros.—Can you prove otherwise ?

Ant.—Can he prove that ?

Pros.—What is your defense ?

Ant.—No more than that I was on the porch
So interested in the passing parade
That I leaned my weight against a cobble
And it fell, with results though not intents,
Similar to those which he discribed.

Char.—Here are more witnesses.   (*Points to Leo. and guards.*)

Abr.—They know no more than you so we
Have no need of them.

Char.—I say he intended to murder me.

(*Enter Hero and Marg., leading Alice.*)

Abr.—You have not proven it.

Hero.—Come quick or we'll be too late.

Alice.—Why in such haste am I brought here ?

Char.—I say he is guilty of treason.

Hero.—I say he is not and I can prove it.

Char.—I say he is guilty and should pay the penalty of death.

Abr.—She says she can prove he is not and conviction goes by
proof alone.   We will hear you.

Hero.—I say he (*pointing to Char.*) is guilty of forming a plot to
ruin Antony.   Here is a woman who o'erheard him, (*to
Alice*).   You tell them, you know it better.

Alice.—What shall I say ?

Hero.—What you told me this morning.

Alice.—I told you nothing.

Char.— She is the prisoner's lover, and this is an excuse for
some advantage.

Hero.—Why, you told me, that Charles and Leopole were plot-
ing to dispose of Antony.

Alice.—If ever I have set my eyes on you before
It has slipped my memory.

Leo. aside.—'Tis wrong for me to be silent.

Char.—This is some ruse to work your pity,
She will weep directly.   I motion for
A death sentence as he is proven guilty.
                    (*Hero places herself beside Antony.*)

Hero.—If he is guilty, then so am 1 as
An accomplice, for I know his mind and
Know it to be as free from treachery
As is God's above.   (*to Alice*)   And you know he is to be
                              (*points to Charles*)
As full of treachery as is a snakes.

Leo. aside.—I must speak.

Char.—That's from the case.   I motion for a sentence.

Abr.—There has been nothing proven in this case,
But I believe,
This lady has some valuable proof
Which she imparted to this other.

Alice.—I know nothing.

Leo.   You lie you do.
And so do I.   Antony, I must speak.
I envied you for defeating me but
Never enough without his aid, (*points to Char.*) to do
What I have done,
He pricked me on with golden promises

'Till I conspired with him to ruin you,
I pushed that cobble from the porch and Charles
Is my accomplice.

Ant.—How about the tie ?

Leo.—   'Twas got by trickery,
Hero is innocent and true to you.

Ant.—Hero, will you forgive
My fickle confidence in you ?

Hero.—I would call nothing fickle'
That was done amid these trials.

(*bells ring twelve.*)

Char. to Abr.—I claim my office, your time's expired.

Abr.—Antony, I find no proof of guilt against you,
So you are discharged.

Char.—Soldiers, he would rob me of my privilege,
This office and this case to finish are mine,
And I'll fight for what is mine.

Ant.—And so will I. (*Rushes out and snatches a sword, meets
Charles, they fight, soldiers drive Leo. and Abr. back with
bayonets. Antony is besting Charles.*)

Char.—Help me, soldiers.

(*Soldiers go to stab Ant. in the back, Hero steps between.*)

Hero.—Away, you cowards from his back !

(*Soldiers stab her, she falls.*) *Ant. stabs Char., turns on
soldiers and drives them back.*)

Hero.—Antony, I hope you think me true,
Good by, good by, Antony. (*dies.*)

(*Antony turns and sees her, throws away his sword and kneels
beside Hero.*)

Ant.—Hero ! Hero ! Dead !
Heaven forgive me for this foul deed,
For I know no sacrifice or penance
With which I may redeem myself.

(*Soldiers stab him in the back, he offers his breast.*)

Here, strike where my mortal source is. and end
My living quick.   Then if my earthly qualities
Of endurance stay with my spirit,
I will o'ertake her.

(Soldiers stab him in the breast.)

Now my Hero,
Your Antony will soon be with you.

(Falls over on Hero and dies.)

(Curtain.)

FISHING FOR FAME.

FISHING FOR FAME.

Now friends, in your conception place yourselves,
In an uptown club, where wealth alone
Has qualities for gaining membership,
Where there's no virtue greater than extravagance,
As all the furnishings do testify;
Such as the walls and ceilings decked with pictures,
That strive with some success, to rival
Old Italian art. With here and there
Large beveled mirrors, of flawless glass, each
The choice of some selected lot, resting
On a wainscoating, of polished rosewood,
That for the beauty of both its knots and grain,
Is nature's masterpiece. Between the ceiling,
And a tall man's hight, there hung a chandelier
Of hand cut glass, upon which height, the artist
Well fulfilled his task, of making it
To outsparkle the stary heavens,
And where artistic taste, would show their beauty
To best advantage, there hung in loops,
Rich draperies, on which, while in a spell,
Some foreign gypsies hand was lead by heaven
While she embroidered them; and for genius
They won the laurels her ambition sought,
Crowning her the queen of needlework.

A masterhand had also, planned and made
The couches and divans which were placed about,
And seemed but as samples of the carpeting,
That yielded at each step, as much as one
Would call a rut upon the highway;
Those without experience, would have
An awkward gate thereon.   Such were the parlors.

Then there was a billiard room, a card room,
A smoking room and a hall for entertainments.
Each as lavishly furnished in its kind.

Tis in the smoking room our scene takes place.
Here were assembled, a half a dozen,
Young and wealthy sports, each with a tale or two,
Of some marvelous or lucky catch,
Of game fish, such as perhaps had happened,
Twice in a hundred expeditions.
But to the inexperienced listener,
It was conveyed as though a common event.

But one listener there; a man of middle age;
Named Smith, of piqued disposition,
With plenty of ambition and a craving
To be famous,one who made it his delight,to slur and try
To level with himself the lucky ones.
One who envied those, who, as he claimed,
Did make a boast,
Of what they had by accident achieved
And would have happened to a truant school boy
Just the same.

                    Then spoke he to the rest:
Is this a quality? is this a gift!
To cast a baited line in the unseen deep
And hane a hungry, brainless fish to chance
Into the trap? If this is an achievement
Worthy of this praise, why: Tom Fool's a hero,
And I would have been, a thousand times,

And my achievements and my name, would be,
A subject for short stories in our magazines,
Or conversation at all social gatherings,
So it shall hereafter, for, hear me boys!
You've bragged of capturing the wiry trout,
The big mouthed pickerel and the strongest bass.
When hunger bade him eat just as your line
Was near.   And for thus capturing a defenseless foe
You pose as heros.   Then so will I!
Who never craved for fame, but such as
To the mighty comes.   For: hear me boys;
When Sol has finished this day at the antipodes,
And sinks himself behind their western limits,
To peep with his familiar, golden fire
Here o'er our eastern hilltops; when he has
To start to-morrow, pierced this heavy vail of night
Enough to make a stream dissernible
I'll have a line therein and try my skill,
And as fishes feed but in the day time
So, after a restless night of fasting
Their appetit is the best.   Now that's a point
You all overlooked but it could not pass my insight.
And by the time you usually cast a line,
When all the fish, have crammed their stommachs
With their natural food and have no appetite,
I'll be returning, with all the hungry ones
That were alert and let my squirming crawler
Tempt them.   I'll prove that I have not lived
To forty-five without experience.
That you knew not of.   For, while you,
Were huddled in a lump between warm sheets,
Perhaps asleep, or, planing the conquest
Of some fair maids heart, or perhaps,
With bandaged brow and ices handy,
To soothe a fever or calm an upset stomach,
You were stealing from the morning,
The few hours sleep you'ld lost the night before
At reveling.   These were the hours I put
To some atvantage.   Many evenings,

Did I assort my tackle, for convienance
And immediate use; and carve such bait
To regular mouthfuls.
As to each certain specie, that I sought,
Was thought to be its favorite morsel.
Thus was I employed.
While you before a glass, were inspecting
Or arranging, some latest style apparal.
Each of us when finished would go our way.
You to shine or be a blunder,
At some social gathering, and I to bed;
To have my regular amount of sleep.
So as to be up and on the way.
Oft in time, to wish you the happy dreams
Which I had had, and you had lost,
During the period of some entertainment,
The charm of which decieved your nature,
To a harmful wakefulness.
And now with drowsy languishness, you slouch
Toward home, while I, with brisk and wakeful stride,
All ambition, make for some dock, or bringe,
Or boat, or anything conveniant.
To those selected spots where fishes feed
'tis keen strategem to always choose aright.
An amature but once in ten times
Strikes it lucky, therefore they condemn the sport.
Gentlemen, not to boast, or try, to crown
Myself with any fickle title, but
All my expeditions were successes
And sent me home o'erburdened. The marketmen,
Would miss my friends those days, for I
Supplied them all. The only thing to mar those trips
Was the lugging coming home. I always,
Strained my sinews to the limit, and oft
A young assistant, to whom I gave a coin
The novice and the seadog hailed me
As their champion, and dunned me for instructions.
When with their knowledge all exhausted,
They had no fish, to me they came for pointers,

Which always brought returns. To-morrow boys,
To prove I am no boaster, I'll make a haul,
Of this same genius fish; the trout,
And my wife's reputation as a cook,
Is current conversation with her friends;
So I will give orders, she shall saison
And prepare, in several ways, to tempt
Your different tastes those selfsame fish,
And you shall be my guest to morrow night.
I will expect you all at eight.   Do you agree ?

After several toasts and wishes of success,
Smith bade them all good night and hurried home
To make his preparation and retire.

Next morning he arose, while darkness still,
Did shade all earthly object with its veil.
Like a harmless barnyarn foul protect its young,
So did the night protect the earth from light.
By charging with its light absorbing body
Upon each artificial ray; as would
Some mighty champion who strove to be supreme.
'Twas a royal battle between light
And darkness.

This did not interest our Smith,
When he'd eaten a few chance morsals;
As there 'was no lingering for a spread,
And gathered up his choicest bait and tackle,
He started out, while night was still supreme
Shielding everything from mortal gaze.

As he trudged along that one hours walk,
That took him to the brook, the gray morning light
The front rank of the day did chance along,
While charging night and all its powers
To a full retreat.   But to even matters,
At the antipodes, night was the master
And had the weak flank of the day in like retreat.

At least of that same traveling, in pouring rain,
Between himself and any kind of shelter.
Still on he trudged for lingering would but
Prolong his torture.

Now and again
He would curse himself for this fool's errand
And vent a curse, on those who praised, this place
As being good for fishing.   And by the time
He had cut his passage to the road
The rain had ceased, the clouds were sinking in the east
And Sol once more shown down in all its splendor;

Without a single fish he started home.
Where he arrived, with aching bones
And rheumatism in every joint;
And a cold that brought on fears of something worse.
But soon his wife, whose every worry was
For his comfort, had bathed each single ache
With balm, and with a women's gentle stroke,
Rubbed through the pores as much as would absorb.
Then tucked him safe in bed.   There he was
When those invited to the feast arrived.

According to a humorous resolution,
They all met at the club, then proceeding
In a body, were ushered to our hero.
Some of them he gently reprimanded
For praising such a place to go for sport,
And to all he took an oath: he would
Never fish again;   So with many wishes
For a speedy recovery they departed.

REMEMBERING

THE

MAINE.

Copyright, 1901, 1905.

BY F. SIMON.

Wonderful are the works of God.
And most wonderful his commonest doings.
Take man himself, where is the work more wonderful.

Here upon this round globe he has placed us,
With different dispositions and ambitions,
To love or hate, to better or break,
Other of his works, and all we must believe
Is for some well meant end. Here he's placed us,
As through adrift, out of his control.
Here one man kills another for a coin.
Another coveting his neighbors wealth.
Here some competing for some other business.
And countries waring for each others power.
Thus on small, medium and larger scales
All is discontent and strife.
Not for what we need, for our wants are small,
But for what we see and our eyes see much.
And what alluring prospect lead us on.
Dreams of wealth and power, for which we'd drudge,
Our whole life long, then to awaken
A common mortal. Tis so with men, concerns
And countries, all striving for some more.

There is one instance chronicled,
In heaven and on earth, where,
Nor power, nor wealth, nor any moit of gain
Would crown the noble souls for risking,
Gun or sabre wounds, pestilence and death.
No grand conquest of arms or diplomacy
Was the goal that put those statemen's genius
To the test, that ranked them with the foremost

Of the world. No prospect of rich mines to sieze.
Or fertile valleys to colonize, with
The roaming populace.
It was not ambition, it was not greed,
 That brought that noble ship (The Maine) to that
Fatal anchorage before Havana.
No, no, but a privilege, by agreement
Twix the powers, that, (a neutral country
Could assist its merchants and their interests,
In a beleagured city.)
Such was the mission of that noble ship,
And thus, not mingling in the strife,
Those brave souls all felt secure. And why not?
Born and nourished in a country, that gives
The men of honor charges of importance.
Why should they even surmize? (That a country
Like Spain, that boasts it was a power,
In the ancient days of Rome's supremacy.
The first country to land, civilized
Human being upon this wilderness.
The foremost country to send its explorers,
Colonizers and missionaries,
To these countries, to teach the savages,)
Would place in the hand of a savage,
The lives of hundreds of human beings.
For such was he, who touched that fatal spring·
That wrecked the Maine, and slaughtered its lusty
Crew as the lay at anchor, guiltless and
· Unsuspecting among the Spanish mines.

Perhaps he thought that these United States
Had but one ship for their sea power,
And in his feverish brain, planned himself
Destined to control their noble navy.
Tis a pity that such pevish brains
Could merit power amongst a nation.

But what must have been the awakening,
When those patriots cried, Halt!
And the disturbed populace was content

For such an avalanche of punishment
Was never dealt to a country before.

Our noble hearted people, already disturbed,
By the reports of Spanish cruelty
To our weak neighbors, needed much less, than
This wholesale murdering of their gallant seamen,

To put them in the frenzy which it did,
But Oh! the wreck and ruin to Spain.
The glory to our statesmenship, and to
Our fighting power. The awakening
Of the world to our untried resources.

No sooner than the echoes of that
Murderous discharge, were swallowed up in space,
And the soaring fragments that were heaved aloft,
One after another from their different heights,
Had dropped and splashed to signal their return.
Before the cloud of smoke, that like a spirit
Rose from the wreck, had drifted out of sight.
All was hustle and hurry for miles around.
For this foul schock, had like an earthquake,
Roused the slumbering people and brought them
From their berths. To the public squares and streets
Where with thumping hearts and trembling nerves,
They met in crowds and questioned one another
Expecting dreadful news. All were alert
And fidgity, from living near the strife.

Not so on board the Maine, where there was danger.
Their each survivor knew his station
And there he stayed. How could he leave?
Seeing one brave lad salute the captain
And report, (The ship was sinking.)
Fear was a word this crew had merely heard of,
And so in order keeping step,
They left the sinking ship as they would have
To a pleasure visit.

But with them came
The tales of horror, that fanned to flames
The slumbering courage in their countrymen's breast.
Each succeeding message bringing detail,
Was as fuel to this patriotic fire,
And as they flashed o'er this broad land, told and retold
In husky voices, they awoke a fury
In our citizens. that naught but war could ease.

Although a faction strove for peace, they could not
Down the people's cry. for (War and vengeance.
Remember the Maine) So war was declared.
A policy much discussed in foreign lands,
That this country, whose army was no more,
Then wandering bands patroling omong
The Indian reservations,
Should challenge the mighty arms of Spain.

When this offend d nation began to muster,
The volunteers in swarms besieged their barracks.
All impatient to avenge, their countries wrong.
Then were our gray haired veterans besieged,
By lusty youths, who where anxious to receive,
Their stowed up kwowledge of the drills,aud everywhere,
In twos and threes, they would shoulder arms, front face
And forward march to his stern command.
This playing soldiers, fired these youthful spirits,
Th seek the stern reality.
From everywhere they came, from cities. towns
And farms. So fast they came the camps looked like
A hurly burly mob, that never could
Be disciplined. But what a change in a few short months.
To see this mob, marching and countermarching
Or wheeling about in companies
Or regiments, without a wave in their straight ranks.
Twas a miracle done with assistance
Of the god of war.

While at home the armies were preparing,
Far off in Hong Kong harbor lay at anchor.
The Pacific Squadron and its crews,
Passing compliments with foreign friends.
'Mid feasting and rejoicing, a message
From home told of the Spanish treachery
To the Maine. A sister ship sent to the bottom,
And hundreds of their comrades murdered
While on a peaceful mission to assist their friends.
Greeted with smiles and courtesy and oppointed,
To an anchorage among the spanish mines,
Their noble hearted comrades, with minds
To pure to conceive such mean advantages,
Were easy victims to this trap.
A threatening murmur among those men
When they heard this news, soon changed to hurrahs
And song as another message followed.
This declaring war was to them more like
An invitation to a feast than bloody combat.
Now could these untried Sailors prove their worth.

    At Manilla Harbor not far off,
In spanish waters, guarded, by spanish
Forts and mines, there lay the enemy, safe
And unassailable, to a timid crew.
But to these men, there lurked a charm in effort.
They sought not for a fallen foe, but one
That could make them strain their wits for victory.

So they set sail for this glorious trip.
Like a picnic party, 'mid song and cheers.
With light hearts they steered their fighting hull,
Through the liquid furrows of the deep
On to Manilla.
Past the forts and mines
Under the veil of night. With not a light
To warn the drowsy Spanish sentinels,
And have them spoil this bit of stratagem.
Not a whisper disturbed the enemy
Until morn, then at a signal

From the Olympia's mast, to open fire,
A dozen cannons roared at once, and sent.
Their iron missiles of death and destruction,
At as many objects from which floated.
The Spanish colors. To rouse them all,
Inviting their full strenght in opposition.

As they peered through portholes and cabin doors,
From watchtowers or over battlements,
Disturbed from heavy slumbers by this rude
Intrusion, yawning and gapping, they beheld
The stars and stripes, and heard from lusty throats,
The battle cry (remember the Maine).
Then in confusion, they started their defense,
Twas to late. For the well directed shots,
From the American ships, had torn large gaps
In their hulls and riggings, and strewn their decks
With silent dead and groaning wounded comrades.
Upsetting order, banishing all control,
Making their different moves conflicting.
And thus confused they were a helpless foe,
Live targets for those well directed shots,
That quenched the life of more than a thousand men.
And battered their ships till they all sank,
With the cost of but one single life.
Well was the Maine remembered at Manilla.

Scattered o'er this broad land, in every state,
Small groups of volunteers did their daily routine
Impatient to amass and strike the foe.
Here they received the news from Manilla,
Praises in colored head lines, mere hints at first,
But followed by the official records,
Of a complete American victory.

The citizens, on hearing the news,
Came to the camps and swelled their rousing cheer.
Everywhere, in cities, towns or hamlets,
They held meetings of appreciation.
With bonfires and fireworks, or passing
Resolutions of praises and thanks.

This double victory, first,
Of the spanish fleet, then a country's praise,
Would make dullest envious, much more
These firy youths, and nothing short of
Leaps and bounds was headway toward meeting the foe.
Caution was tedious and loudly condemned.
From lowest to highest this spirit prevailed,
The spirit that makes success.

Now were the drills more early,
The inspections more exact   The soldiers
More attentive.   The officers more alert.
All seeking some means of improvement.
Not even the higher departments,
Were free from this contagion, there to
New life was infused, making them cheerful
And confident and with mighty heaves from
The highest to the lowest as a man
Were the preparations hastened, to equip
The needed force to embark for Cuba
And whip those guilty of the Maine's sad fate

Now was each drill hailed as the final.
Each arrival of equipments, arms or
Ammunition.   The transports reported
As waiting, while rumors for starting, named
Every hour for a week.

Each day in service is divided,
With the exactness of the sun, naming
Certain hours for leisure, and not to know
Those hours now would mean to choose them as
The hardest.   Not a soul but was pawing
His effects, culling his choicest trinkets,
Trading keepsakes or wistfully discarding

All over a stinted weight.   Twas like a
Busy day in some large industry, where,
Each has his mind intent, on adding
His little mite to the one grand whole.

Far famed are the southern states for sunny days
Twas on one of the finest they had ever had,
That the army awoke, had mess and assembled.
When they heard the command of : *Forward March*
Loud and clear, then with all their pride and pains
Did these different companies move.
Like so many solid masses, borne on
Conveyances, so perfect was their manœuvering.
  Now was the harmony
Between, the different branches well displayed.
The army, a mighty host of boyant spirits,
Proud of their might and anxious to display it.
The navy appearing like so many
Awkward, bulky hulls (but fitted with equipments.
That controlled them on the seas, as smooth and gentle
As caresses) and the fleet of transports
A queer assortment of crafts, as though, one
From every model were sent in competition.
Three seperate forces each subject to
An independent leader, straining every nerve
To fulfill orders and anxious for success.

Tis an old remark, (The sight of a lifetime)
But in those southern ports there now took place,
A sight not met with in a thousand lifetimes.
Steamers and barges riding on the tides.
Tossing and tugging at their anchorage,
Like unruly puppies imposing on
A timid master. Palacial yachts
And liners, striped of their beauty, to be
Of better service, while just beyond them
Guarding the harbour, rode the ironclads.
With a bold and threatening confidence.
The army coming aboard.   To the novice

They appeared a mob, but known to themselves,
By divisions and sub-divisions, down to
The smallest group, and, as when a boulder
That the weathers of ages upon ages
Had loosened, in one unbroken mass, bounds andre bounds
To the valley below and leaves the mount unmoved.
Thus did each company at a call,
Leave the ranks to be ushered to their berths.
This was a sight that thrilled the blood, and put a bloom
On the pale cheeks of many a sickly youth
Who had been rejected.

When all were aboard, prepared for every possible hitch
That forethought could invent; What a din was raised.
Steam whisles blowing to every pitch,
Druming and fifing and bands a playing,
The people shouting and waving adieus,
Boys with their noisiest toys and trinkets;
The tin can brigade; that's cursed and snailed at
By the nervous, were now the heros
This was the scene as the army left for
Cuba.

Such a fearless and careless group,
Had ne'r before taken passage. There they were
In those frail hulls; frail compaired to men or war,
Steering direct to the enemy's stronghold,
With it's danger of traps, as mines in the seas,
Masked batterys along shore, or by chance
To meet the enemy's fleet.
Neither in their looks or actions was there
A hint of fear, fear for dangers to come.
Amusement or excitement was their object.
And where two boats, nose to nose, were having
A friendly encounter of speed, twould draw
A crowd that gave their judgement, by derisively
Jeering the looser, though the margin were but a foot.
Groups collected at every upstart.
As a song or a dance or a trial

Of skill or endurance. Thus with no thought
Of their safety, but relying on those
In command did they sail this venturesome voyage.
Not an incident with enough importance,
To be known beyond the office, marred
The trip up to landing. Then came their need
Of cleverness. For every harbour, every inlet,
Where it was possible to land was well defended.

Allthough not forwarned, more than by forethought,
They arrived forearmed, knowing the enemy
To be alert for any mode of attack
Undaunted by opposition they went ahead
Straining with recklessness the bounds of safety.
Peering incivilly into the enemy's affairs.
Searching the shore above and below
For a place to force a landing in spite of
The enemy's advantage.

Eager to act and confident, they soon
Made a choice, and in counsel determed their course.
With wavering signals was each ship instructed.
When all were ready up went the signal
(Move as ordered) and as when a herd
Of timid sheep, startled while grazeing
Scatter aimlessly, so the ships, some up,
Some down, baffling the ancious foe
Drawing them from here to there and back again,
By assembling at different places,
Feigning to land, far from where they intended.

When their ruse had succeeded, selected leaders
At a signal, with ships equiped and crews
Instructed, against all foreseen obstacles,
Boldly charged the coveted landing.
Twas no modern city with docks and piers
For convienance, but to shallow water
Then swimming or wading to shore, while some,
Skilled marksmen, overawed the weak and baffeled garri-
With a firing so accurate, that   (son

When a shot missed, twas by a margin so small,
When whistling by its intended victim,
Twould make him dodge and try to avoid,
The bullet that had passed him by a rod.
By surmounting such obstacles, they gained
A foothold, the object of this bold stroke.

Though what was done so far was much, twas but
The beginning. Twas as when a hungry lion,
Spies a straggling wolf and with one bound, secures
That dainty morsel. Then a dieing yelp
Brings round the pack, changing the lions position,
From easy master to the defensive.
Then are his qualities called upon.
Then does he deeds of death and carnage.
As with one stroke of his mighty paw
Snapping the spine of one that had ventured,
Within the bounds of his reach, or with his
Massive jaws, crushing a skull to pulp
Unmindful of their struggles and howling
Then tossing them aside, intent upon
The next until he has downed all opposition
To his feast. 'T is from such victories as these
He is known as king of beasts. As with the lion,
So was it with the Americans now.
Through their own cunning they had tricked the enemy,
To expose a certain landing, then taken
Possession in it's weakness, thus robbing
The enemy of half it's power; and
As they realized this staggering blow,
Chagrined and furious, they arrayed themselves
In opposition; changing the American's
Position, from easy masters to the defensive.
This put their fighting qualities to the test.
And as the lion they enacted,
Deeds of bravery, skill and cunning.
Crowing all with a victory.

As was natural for a time, all was
Topsy turvy. Food, arms and equipments

All in a heap, men and companys
Scattering aimlessly.   But the hustling
And ambitious spirits, prevailing among
These men soon brought this chaos into order
As smooth as a model household the pride
Of a loving wife.

             But war was just beyond.
War with all it's horrors, it's noise and confusion,
It's wounds and amputations, its fevers
And death.   Of all the afflictions borne by
This earth inhabitants, war is the worst.
Plagues und famines, cyclones and eruptions,
Are beyond control but war is of mans
Own making.   Men with reason, God's noblest work,
Man who in pity, would sunder two fighting curs
Yet they themselves, trained and practiced, in
The surest way of killing one another.
Or win praises and honor for planning
The move or weapen that will do the most harm.

     Nations have their rise and fall as well as men.
And as they rise they're confident and strong
And opposition to their onward march,
Is but a spur to glory, but past the climax
And declining, all is blunders and weakness.
So was it now with Spain.   Her glories fading,
Her power loosing hold, opposed by a
Rising nation with dash and confidence
Before which they wilted, steadily retreating
To their stronghold, where, without a siege, almost
Without a strugle tney surrendered,
Leaving the Americans in control.

           Thus far, the glories
Attained in the struggle for Cuba, went
To the armies, now come the navies for
Their share.   The government in Spain, knowing
Their armies plight in Cuba, sent a squadron

To their aid. Now be it luck or destiny
Or what it will, but the Spanish admiral
Through his own cleverness was defeated.
For clever it surely was, to trick
The American patrol, and gain
The harbour where their armies lay. But twas
His downfall. The American army
Controling on land and the powerful
Ships before the harbour, had so cornered
The Spanish fleet, the best they could wish for
Was to escape.

Thus they stood, day succeeded day without
A suspicious move. The trapped ones, anciously
Expecting a glimmer of hope, wishing
Some miracle, would, if only for
The shortest spell, confuse the guard before
The harbour, their only road to liberty.
But no, their vigilance to be free was
No more thorough, than was their guards to capture
Things seemed at a standstill, but only seemed.   (them
The army was preparing to harrass
The imprisoned fleet, cautiously advancing,
From mound to mound, becoming so threatening,
That to remain meant sure distruction, while
In flight there seemed a glimmer of hope.
But never did a hungry beast, couch and wait
More patiently for it's favorite morsel.
Than did the American guard before
The harbour.   Not a speck, or a ripple,
Within these bounds escaped their notice
So diligent was the guard.
The strict routine with the unchanging scene
Was tiring the patients of these brave men,
Used to changes, to seeing the world.
When one bright morning, a cry from the watch.
Ship Ahoy ! In the harbor there. They're coming out !
Like a magic wand in fairie tales,
Turned these men into fighting demons.

Now all was hustle and expectation.
Surmising the plans of the enemy.
As also the best means to oppose them.
Straight at them came the Spanish fleet, as though
To ram, to charge their bulky hulls head on,
To test their beams and armour and leave the honors
To the shipright, or, perhaps to mingle
Hull to hull in deadly combat and win
Or lose decide supremacy then and there.
But no! They steer to starboard, thus revealing,
Their plans was to escape if possible.

With a base on which to plan their battle,
The tension on these men relaxed, the tension,
Caused by doubt and anxiety. The doubt
The whole worlds in, of what good or ill may
Befal us this next instant, and the anxiety
To meet it succesfully.

The signals
Waved for battle and from the merry way
These tars, heaved at a chain or a rope,
To hasten the start, bespoke no danger
In the coming conflict although they knew
It meant: win or die!

With a whirling and churning in the rear,
Out shot these ponderous hulls; slowly at first,
But gaining every minute. Straight at the foe,
In a threatening way. Like some mighty champion,
Who, while dallying with an easy opponent,
Receives a chafning blow, then straight his honor pric-
He falls to like one inspired.   (ked,
How the fires were fed and nursed,
As the orders came below: to crowd on steam.
Until at every turn of the wheel,
It seemed the joints would sunder.

Now and then,
A deafening boom from a heavy gun;

L. of C.

To try the distance as they drew nearer,
Would bring all eyes towards the foe, to know,
Did it hit, or splash before or beyond them.
The first splash beyond the foe, was the signal,
To open fire; Promptly obeyed almost
By every gun at once. From the turrets,
The decks and it seemed from every loophole,
Streaks of fire and clouds of smoke shot out,
Laden with iron missiles, of death and
Destruction. While the force that sent them on
Their journey, left a recoil, that it seemed,
No bolts or mortise could withstand.

Both fleets were now sailing at topmost speed,
Steadily firing. The Spanish, more to
Check the Americans, while the Americans
Were intent on winning. Thus on they fought.
Sometimes in a lull, taking careful aim
With a mighty gun, and firing singly,
So but little smoke would hinder watching
It's effect Then firing broadsides, volley
After volley, while for smoke, nothing was
Dissernable across the ship. Still they fired.
One would think at random. Then another lull.
And as they emerged from the vail of smoke
And peered across the water, from a ship
Just opposite, a cloud of smoke rose heavenward
And flying fragments filled the air.
She's wounded! was the cry, as she, keeling,
Was steering for shallow water with her colors
Slowly coming down.

The good, the migthy, those worthy
Of supremacy, be it one person,
A group or a multitude; are as gentle,
As lovable and as sympathetic,
As they are strong, and although while battling
For a just cause, they will punish with all
Their might, when the battle is over they will

Minister to the fallen with the self same ardor;
Such were the Americans.   And where
The enemy's signal meant distress, they
Lay by, to aid and comfort them as friends.
Here was an event.   These bitter enemies
Of an hour ago, now anxious for
Each others comfort.   While yet in sight,
Friends of both were battling in bitterest
Enmity.

The Spaniards fought desperately, but their shots
Went wide of the hulls intend, dropping
Harmlessly into the sea.   While the Americans,
Almost unharmed themselves, had crippled a ship,
Growing bolder, and drawing nearer, until
Every shot seemed to rip it's self, into
A Spanish hull.

The little spark of hope
The Spaniards had, that chance or luck might aid them
Was growing dim, and gloomy were their spirits.
As the Americans, flushed with confidence,
Bore down upon them, ripping aud tearing
Their hulls to pieces, until, one after another,
They all surrendered. crippled and helpless.

Thus ended the battle, made so vicious
By the men in remembrance of their comrades,
The victims of the Maine.